CW00516124

ARMY DAYS

Reuben Cole, The Early Years Book 2

STUART G YATES

CHAPTER ONE

He was dreaming. Back at the ranch, running through the fields, his mother close behind shouting with joy for him to slow down. If anything, this spurred him on, and he was sprinting; arms and legs pumping, head thrown back, eyes closed, luxuriating in the sheer pleasure of being alive. He didn't see the fallen tree until he was upon it, and he tripped and fell headfirst into the ground. Rolling over and over, his mother's concerned voice calling him as he tumbled, "Wake up, Cole! Wake up!"

Reuben Cole sprang awake and sat up, startled, but instantly alert. The big, cheery face of Sergeant Burnside filled his immediate line of vision. Sergeant Burnside, who had guided him during the enlistment process, helping him to find his way around the camp, smiled broadly. Cole had spent an uncomfortable night on a makeshift camp-bed inside a large tent. "Get your things together and I'll take you over to your barrack room. That's where you'll be staying from now on."

The two men marched across the parade ground, the sun nothing more than a smudge in a misty-grey dawn. Already, Cole found himself shivering in his thin, threadbare shirt. "Quartermaster will fit you out with extra clothing," said Burnside, giving

Cole the once-over. "It'll be blazing hot in a few hours, but these early mornings are chilly, as is the night. You should forever be prepared, soldier."

Stopping abruptly before a long line of nondescript wooden huts, Burnside pointed across to the entrance to one of them. "That's yours. Come on, I'll take you to meet your companions."

" 'Morning, gentlemen," said Burnside, and introduced Cole to two rough-looking types lounging on the steps of the first hut. They were dressed in buckskin clothes and slouch hats, guns tied down at their hips.

"This here is Alvin Cairns and Augustus Renshaw," said Burnside. "They are from Kansas and are the best-damned trackers we have. You stick close to them and learn what you can. You won't go far wrong that way, Reuben. Believe you me."

That was the last time Burnside ever called him Reuben. From now on, he was Private Cole, foraging scout for Company D of the 10th United States Infantry Regiment out of Pennsylvania.

Cole snapped to attention and gave a rigid, well-drilled salute. Burnside smiled, casually returned the salute, and strode off.

"He must like you," drawled Cairns, cutting off a hunk of chewing tobacco from a pouch he kept at his waist. "Ain't ever seen him look so cheerful. Ain't that right, Augustus?"

"Sure is."

"Get yourself some food young fella. Load your guns, and make sure you have plenty of water. Maybe a coat or something to keep you warm. We is going for a ride."

"Wait a minute," said Cole, quickly. "Going for a ride? Where to?"

"You'll see soon enough."

"But, I've only just got here. I need time to get to know everything and everyone. Besides, we can't just ride out of here without telling anyone!"

"You think we is idiots, squirt?"

"Yeah," piped up Renshaw, "is that it? You think us is idiots?"

"I never said that," protested Cole, looking from one snarling face to another. "I'm just making sure, that's all."

"Making sure?" Cairns laughed, a grating, mocking sound. "Who do you think you are, squirt?"

"Yeah, who do you think you are?"

Cole was about to say something, bring up the obvious point that Augustus Renshaw, his big, lanky frame towering over him, was nothing but an echo of his associate Cairns, when he decided against such an action. These men looked and were dangerous. Each sported a brace of Navy Colts and bore a grizzled look. It seemed clear to Cole that these men were seasoned killers, quick to violence. Burnside had hinted that Cairns was a skilful tracker. Renshaw, however, remained something of a mystery. For one thing, he appeared clean, which was rare for any soldier, let alone a scout who spent most of his time out on the plains. Perhaps Cole should ask around the barracks, find out about their reputation, and discover if they were men not to be crossed. Until then, he decided to keep his mouth closed.

"Get your stuff from your bunk, squirt," said Cairns. "And, in the future, you just do as you're told. No more questioning my authority."

Cole nodded once, avoiding Cairn's icy glare. Before he stomped out, the tracker spat out a long line of tobacco juice, which barely missed Cole's boot. Renshaw giggled.

"I didn't mean nothing by it," said Cole, quietly, thinking it best to offer up some sort of explanation.

Renshaw tilted his head. "Just get your stuff."

"I wouldn't want you to think I am – damn it, I'm sorry is what I'm trying to say."

Renshaw's hand moved in a blur, striking Cole resoundingly across the cheek. Cole reeled to the side, the blow so powerful it felt as if it almost tore his head off.

"Don't cuss," said Renshaw, and left, leaving Cole to clutch at his smarting face, eyes wet with the shock of the assault.

3

Stepping inside his barrack room, he avoided the questioning stares of his fellow soldiers, most of whom were young recruits like himself.

"What happened to you?" one young recruit asked, sitting on his bunk adjacent to Cole's. He was busily polishing his boots, which looked as if they were about to fall apart.

Unconsciously, Cole brushed the back of his hand against his cheek. It felt hot to the touch. "Ah, nothin'."

"Sergeant Burnside stored your equipment under your bed," said the recruit. He struck out a hand. "Name's Andrew Stamp."

"Pleased to meet you," said Cole, relieved to find a friendly face.

Smiling, Cole reached under his bunk and pulled out his bedroll. Inside, wrapped in an oily cloth, was the handgun his father had presented to him on the morning he left the ranch. It was an eighteen-fifty-eight Remington-Beals Army revolver, his father's pride and joy, and he insisted Reuben take it rather than the bulky Colt Dragoon he'd acquired. "I'll take this old dependable as back-up," he'd told his father.

Now, crouching down, weighing the Remington in his hands, he knew he needed to travel light. He left the Dragoon behind, gathered up his blanket and canteen, and tipped his hat towards Stamp. "I'll be gone for a few days," he said.

"Action? You going into action? Damn, that makes me jealous."

"Wouldn't be too anxious about getting into a scrape," interjected another recruit, a powerfully built fellow who strolled over to them. "Heard from some other fellas that the army lost a lot of buddies last time they mixed it with the Rebs. Said the safest place to spend any time during a war is in the bunkhouse."

"Not sure the colonel would agree," said Stamp, returning to his polishing. "Where is it you're going?"

Cole shrugged. "Don't know. My immediate superior has all of that information. I'm just a 'squirt', or so he keeps telling me."

"Is that Cairns, the tracker?" asked the big one.

4

"Yeah. You know him?"

"I know of him. Saw him take apart two regulars a couple of weeks ago. That man is mean, mean and as hard as nails. I have never seen anyone move and swing punches the way that man did. Laid 'em both out cold, one of 'em with a broken jaw. Best just keep your head down and do as he says."

"I reckon you're right," said Cole. He gave them both a parting smile and went out into the sunlight to find the quarter-master's office and choose himself a coat.

CHAPTER TWO

They did not halt on that first day. Sauntering along, all three with their hat brims pulled down as protection from the unrelenting sun, they finally camped down by a small brook just as evening drifted into night. Underneath some willow oaks, they sat and munched down a selection of corn biscuits and hard-tack. "I'll make coffee in the mornin'," said Renshaw, but nobody was listening. Exhausted from a long day in the saddle, each man settled down and soon the only sound was that of their snoring. "I guess I'll take first watch too," he said and slowly rolled himself a cigarette.

It seemed to Cole he had barely closed his eyes when strong, insistent fingers gripped hold of his collar and shook him awake.

"Cole," hissed Renshaw. "We got company."

Scrambling to his feet, Cole instinctively reached for his Remington-Beals and whispered, "Who? Where?"

"Yonder," said Renshaw. He was nothing but a dark grey smudge against the darkness of the night, so Cole could not make out his expression. There was no disguising the concern in his voice, however.

"Have you roused Cairns?"

"Cairns has gone."

"Gone?" Cole grabbed hold of Renshaw's arm and hauled himself to his feet. "What do you mean, gone?"

"What I say. Told me he was going to relieve himself – his words, not mine. I thought nothing of it at first, but he has been gone too long. Then, I heard horses. A few, I reckon. Maybe six. Smelled 'em, too. They is Rebs, I reckon."

"Augustus, we need to get the hell away from here. We can't go up against six or more Rebs. They must have already taken out Cairns. We'll slip away, real quiet-like."

"What in the hell are you talkin' about, you mealy-mouthed coward? I ain't leaving Cairns behind, no way!"

He tore himself free of Cole's grip and drew his own handgun. "You run if you want to, you bastard, but I ain't going anywhere until I have found Cairns."

"I ain't running anywhere, damn you. What I mean is, we should return to the camp and get more men."

"I said no cussin'!"

The hand came around again, but this time, Cole was ready. He blocked the blow with his left arm and, with the other, rammed the barrel of his gun under Renshaw's chin. "You try that again and I'll blow your damned head off."

Renshaw's eyes flashed white in the gloom. "You better mean what you say, squirt, or I'll be doing the same to you."

Cole felt Renshaw's gun prod into his midriff. He groaned. "I ain't the pushover you think I am, I promise you that. We'll settle this afterwards, once we've found Cairns."

"All right, but settle it we will, I promise you that."

The pressure in his gut eased as Renshaw withdrew. Cole grunted and dropped his gun into its holster. "Seeing as you won't do the sensible thing, let's try and figure out from which direction them riders is coming, then we'll flank 'em and see if we can even up the odds a little."

They quietly slipped off into the dark. Within a couple of

dozen paces, Cole had lost Renshaw in the night, his figure blending in amongst the surrounding trees. Kneeling, he squeezed his eyes shut and did his best to better adjust his eyes to the gloom. When he opened them again, he could make out a little more, but not much. The smell of horse sweat and leather, however, was closer than it had been. He made out some rocks and got down behind them, gun in hand.

The riders appeared like phantoms, grey-clad riders moving forward with extreme care. Cole made out their hats, the carbines in their arms, and then, as they drew ever closer, their voices.

"I told you they was here. Not far now."

Cole frowned, straining his ears to hear.

"We have to find 'em," came the responding drawl of a Texan. "If they report back that they have found our camp, it'll put paid to our plans."

"We'll find 'em. If I know Augustus, he'll be fast asleep dreaming of his momma's home-cooking."

Some of the men sniggered.

Cole rolled away, pressing his back against the rock, and almost screamed out his frustration. It was Cairns. He was leading those Rebs towards Cole and Renshaw to kill them both before they ever got the chance to discover anything about the Rebs' whereabouts. There were no other scouts in camp and, after getting rid of Cole and Renshaw, with Cairns being the only one, he could lead the Union troops a merry-dance. Meanwhile, the Rebs would manoeuvre to their rear, and all of General McClellan's plans for routing the Confederates around the Rappahannock River would be lost. It was clear, to Cole at least, that the only course left was to get back to camp and warn the others. Persuading Renshaw might prove the most difficult part, however. The man seemed to have an unnatural attachment to Cairns; more like a doting dog than a companion on the trail. Perhaps there was something in their shared past that made them so close? Had Cairns saved his life, got him out of some bad scrapes, ensured he continued with his role as army scout when Renshaw appeared to have had the most limited skills? There had to be something.

Before Cole could reach any meaningful conclusion, the rustle of trampled down undergrowth made him sit up. He slowly drew and cocked his revolver. He squinted into the night, hardly daring to breathe. They must have somehow caught wind of his presence. Swallowing down his fear, for he knew beyond any doubt that if they caught him, they would kill him, Cole gathered himself in preparation to shoot it out.

"Cole? Damn it, where are you?"

Cole let out a long sigh. It was Renshaw scrambling around in the dark. "Here," he hissed. "And, for God's sake, keep your voice down."

Renshaw crawled closer, breathing hard. "I thought I'd never find you." He squashed himself against the rock. "They've moved on, so don't worry none. I think they're making towards our camp. Don't know how they—"

"Augustus, you need to listen to me. What I'm about to tell you is going to surprise you."

"What? You mean about Cairns?"

Cole felt his heart skip a beat. He reeled back in shock. "You mean, you *know*?"

"Of course I know, you idiot! I wasn't sure of you, not until just now, so that is why I had to maintain this charade of the backwoods' fool. I am what is termed in polite circles as a spy."

"A spy? You mean ...?"

"I mean I work undercover for the Federal government. We've known for some time Rebel infiltrators were working behind our lines, gathering information on the Major-General's plans to outwit General Johnston. Cairns is part of such a network, and now I have the proof."

"We're gonna capture him?"

"Cole, he ain't the sort of man you take prisoner, not without a fight. No, my job is to kill him and then round up the others as best I can. Those who accompany him, and the rest back in camp."

"But, you can't just kill him, Augustus! That's tantamount to murder."

"What is you, Cole, a Sunday stay-at-home preacher or what? I know you is young, so I will give your opinion due consideration because of that, but we're fighting a war! We will use *any* means available to undermine and defeat our enemy."

"Including assassination?"

"Including *whatever it takes*! Now, come on. If we're quick, we can outflank 'em and bring such a fire down upon them they will believe an entire company is assailing their sorry asses."

CHAPTER THREE

The riders lit torches as they searched fruitlessly for the remnants of Cole and Renshaw's camp. Crackling through the gloom, the sound of their frustrated voices could be clearly heard, with Cairn's voice constantly urging and reassuring them. As they listened, Renshaw's hand curled around Cole's forearm, gripping him hard. "Damn it, I hate that man."

"Don't cuss, Augustus."

Cole heard the violent intake of breath. His companion did not appreciate his sarcasm. "You shut your mouth, squirt, because you ain't funny. Concentrate and be serious. Those burning torches have lit up their position beautifully. We can easily get around them. I shall move across to their rear as you take up a position in their flank. As soon as I open up, you do the same."

"You think that's the best way, Augustus? There is half a dozen of 'em, and I reckon they is fairly good at what they do – killing."

"I aim to put Cairns in the ground, squirt. You do as I say and all will be well. I have a brace of Navy Colts that will serve me well enough. I left my Henry back in our camp. If I get the chance, I will circle back to find it. If they take our horses, we is doomed."

"I, too, have a carbine in the camp. We should have waited, made a stand there."

"Always wisest after the event, ain't yeh, squirt?" He hawked and spat into the ground. "Let's get this done. Remember, you wait for my signal."

With that, he disappeared into the night, moving with surprising nimbleness. Watching him go, Cole felt his stomach clenching and the sweat sprout across his forehead. When he checked the Remington's load, his hands shook uncontrollably. The situation reminded him of what happened when he and Henderson, his father's bodyguard from those early years, went up against a bunch of killers. They fared badly that day. Would it be the same now? He had no way of knowing, so he sat and tried to settle his nerves... turn his mind to more pleasant things. None of it worked. The longer he sat, the more his stomach flipped. The bile rose into his throat, and for a moment, he thought he would be sick. Swallowing it down, he suppressed a cough, clambered to his feet, and moved in what he hoped was a parallel direction with the riders.

Within a few short steps, it became clear that he was in danger of losing his way. The burning torches faded away into the distance, and the smell of the horses and constant chatter of the riders all became nothing more than a memory. Floundering, his eyes darted this way and that. Panic gripped him, and the more he searched and failed, the more desperate he became. Breaking out into a wild, ill-directed run, he bounded over fallen trees and rocks, tramping carelessly through the undergrowth, all the while straining to hear but picking nothing up.

As he burst out from a tangle of bushes and smaller trees, he ground to a halt, his eyes wide, doing his utmost to pick out any detail. The realisation of his stupidity dawned on him too late. It was no wonder he could no longer see the torches. The riders, all but one of whom were now dismounted, had extinguished them sometime before. Now, they stood, their handguns primed and ready, all pointing to Cole as he fumbled into the clearing. The star-speckled sky allowed him to see the details. Of all of them, the one man who took all of his attention sat on his horse, hands on the pommel, laughing helplessly. "Dear God Almighty, if it ain't the squirt! Take hold of him, boys, but be careful mind, he is a wildcat, that one is!" More cackling laughter accompanied his words, and Cole felt himself sinking into an open pit of despair.

Rough hands seized him, and he was dragged forward through the scrub to his former camp. They threw him to the ground, one of the men holding Cole's Remington aloft. "My, this is a beauty," he chirped, much to the amusement of his companions. "I'll take this as my trophy."

Sprawled on his back and propped up by his elbows, Cole watched them in disgust as they led their horses to the trees and secured them there. Last to enter was Cairns, who idly slipped from his saddle and swaggered across to where Cole was. His teeth flashed white in the gradually retreating night. Within the hour, Cole calculated, dawn would turn the night sky to grey, and a new day would bring with it a whole host of new problems. If only Renshaw would make his play perhaps then the balance could be tipped.

"Well, well, squirt. Fancy seeing you again."

Cole climbed to his feet, unconsciously dusting off the dirt from his pants. "To hell with you, Cairns. You traitorous son of a —" From nowhere, one of the Rebs dashed forward and cracked a fist across Cole's jaw, flattening him to the ground where he writhed, clutching his face, the pain burning as if he were on fire.

"Hold your tongue, boy," spat the Reb. "The only traitor here is you!"

"Easy now, Mal," said Cairns, getting down on his haunches. "He's a boy learning what he can about the great outdoors. He has no understanding of the ways of men or war."

13

"That ain't no reason to go spouting lies and inaccuracies, Cairns. Let's string him up."

"No, no, let's just wait a short while, Mal. Boy, where is Augustus?"

They beat him when he did not answer, two of the others holding him between them, a third slamming fists into his guts, ribs and face from fists encased in leather gloves. Several of the blows were delivered with such force that they almost felled Cole, despite the men holding him. His mouth filled with blood, teeth cracked, eyes sank into swiftly swelling flesh. His cheekbones screamed with the agony created by so many well-delivered punches. Somewhere in his scrambled mind, he recalled the beating he'd taken from Jess, one of his father's cowhands. This was far worse.

"All right," he heard Cairns saying from a distance. "He ain't gonna tell. Let him go."

The men duly dropped him, and the next sensation that invaded Cole was the bitter, dry taste of hard earth in his mouth as he fell headfirst to the ground, all strength gone. But, not his resistance. He was damned if he'd tell them anything. Through the swirling red mist before his eyes, he was vaguely aware of feet moving around him, raucous shouts and the one called Mal shouting, "Let's string him up!"

It was as if he'd slipped into a dream. He was aware of men picking him up, lashing his wrists together behind his back, lifting him onto the back of a horse. There was much shouting and laughing, and perhaps that was the figure of Cairns standing in front of him, arms folded across his chest, that mocking laugh so recognisable. But, he no longer cared. His body was awash with pain, senses in shreds. All he longed for was sleep, blessed rest, an end to the ignominy of such a defeat.

He jerked himself awake when they put the rope around his neck, the rough fibres cutting into his neck, and he kicked and struggled. All of it was useless, of course. There was no escape, the inevitability of his dreadful doom gripping him with indescribable terror. His young life, barely begun, extinguished at the end of a rope... lynched. Not even the morality of a trial. Only to swing from a tree branch alone, forgotten, easy pickings for the crows. He railed at the injustice of it. Feverishly, he wriggled, pulled and twisted his body in increasingly useless attempts to set himself free. All his efforts were in vain, and he cried out, "You villains, you murderers! You'll pay for this, all of you. In the fires of Hell, you'll—"

"Pipe down, boy," snapped Cairns, and raised his pistol. "Say good morning to your maker." He eased back the hammer of his gun in preparation to shoot and send the horse beneath Cole galloping forward.

CHAPTER FOUR

From his vantage point a few paces away, Renshaw lay amongst a thick cluster of gorse. He'd managed to circle the group, and had retrieved his Henry. He now had the men in his sights, the quickly lightening sky allowed him to make the group out much more clearly than would have been the case only ten minutes or so before. He watched everything... the way they beat Cole, how he held out and didn't utter a single word despite the viciousness of the blows. The boy had sand, of that there could be no mistaking. He did not deserve to die like this, at the end of a lynch mob's rope.

As Cairns raised his pistol, Renshaw drew in a breath and squinted down the barrel of his rifle. The revolver exploded, the horse bolted and Cole began his grotesque death dance. Renshaw took careful aim and fired.

The single-shot severed the rope supporting Cole, who plummeted to the ground, rubber legs collapsing under him.

He lay in the dirt, not aware of much. Voices. Gunshots. Horses bucking, screaming. All of it a confusion of noise with no real substance. Pandemonium, in other words. His jangled senses battled to try and gain some awareness. His body was alive with pain, especially his jaw, which he believed was broken. The only thought that registered with any substance was a simple one, but enormous in its implications – he was alive!

With his senses recovering, albeit slowly, he knew he must find his gun. But, where to look? All around him, men were scrambling about, losing off shots into the surrounding bush. By now, the morning was well up, the sun already blistering, and visibility was good, except that nobody seemed to know from where the firing was coming. It struck Cole that whoever assaulted the group of men knew exactly what they were doing, always moving, shooting, then disappearing into cover.

One of the riders threw up his arms and fell backwards over a clump of rock, quite dead. As he slid to the ground, Cole took his chance and managed to sway across to the corpse. Desperately, he took up the dead man's revolver and turned just in time to see Cairns, face alive with fury, aiming straight at him.

Cole launched himself to the side just moments before two bullets smacked into the rock and ricocheted away. He rolled over and over, doing his best to keep moving, but Cairns, too, was moving, fanning his revolver as he did so. The bullets flew harmlessly by, giving Cole enough time to rise on one knee, take careful aim, and shoot Cairns in the leg. He squawked and fell, clutching at the wound and the pulsing blood squirting through his fingers.

More shots. Another of the riders fell. Several men screamed. Cole got down behind the rock again and eased off another round, hitting a rider in the right shoulder. The gun fell from the man's numbed hand and he dropped, hands clasping together, pleading for his life. His companions were slowly withdrawing, firing haphazardly in all directions, with the stench of cordite thick in the air, and clouds of black powder smoke hitting the back of the throat. In that small, contained area, there seemed to be no respite from the chaos all around them.

Suddenly, the remaining riders were making a break for it, thrashing through the trees to find their horses. Cole slumped down on his backside and watched them retreat. Only the wounded rider remained, eyes streaming with tears, mouth trembling... "Please, for the love of God..."

Ignoring him, Cole checked his gun and found it to be empty. He threw it away in disgust and was about to go in search of another when Renshaw came out of his cover, methodically cleaning out one of his Colt Navies. He stepped up to the kneeling rider and shook his head. "Boy, you've got to shut up with that whining."

With infinite calmness, Renshaw re-primed his gun, gave the cylinder a flamboyant twirl, and shot the quivering rider through the head without so much as a blink.

Cole gaped in disbelief, not able to find the strength to move or speak.

Ignoring him, Renshaw looked around the remnants of the camp. "Where's Cairns?"

Even if he had wanted to, Cole could not find the strength to speak. Renshaw had cold-bloodedly murdered the rider, a man who had plainly surrendered. All rules of war told him that if a combatant surrendered, then he should be taken in as a prisoner. What Renshaw had done brought a knot of disgust and anger to his guts.

"You bastard," Cole hissed, getting to his feet.

Renshaw's fist erupted into his face, launching him backwards. He fell to the ground with a sickening, solid thump, and lay there dazed. "You watch your mouth, boy. Now, I asked you a question – where is Cairns?"

Propping himself on his elbows, Cole sniffed up a trickle of blood from his nose, hawked and spat it out. "I shot him. I think he got away."

"Well, ain't that just dandy, you dumb-ass. The whole point of this was to bring him to justice, and you, you fairy-assed useless piece of cow-dung, you let him go?" Shaking his head, Renshaw took to searching the camp for anything he could salvage. "We need our horses," he muttered to himself. "We have a long ride back to the camp, and if we don't find those horses, it'll take us weeks. You hear me, boy? *Weeks.*"

Cole stood up and allowed his eyes to settle on the dead rider. "Why did you kill him?"

"He was a Reb. He was here to kill us."

"But, he'd surrendered, damn your eyes!"

A black shadow fell across Renshaw's face. "You keep talking like that, boy, and the next bullet I fire goes straight into your heart."

"Another murder?"

"No one will question the fact that you died under enemy fire, so you just keep talking and you'll soon be snuggling up nice and cosy with your new-found friend there."

Cole was about to speak when he noted Renshaw's grip around the butt of his revolver tightening. Taking a deep breath, he decided against making any more comments. Besides, he felt dreadful. The pounding in his head from receiving so many blows was almost unbearable. In the frenzy of the firefight, he'd forgotten the beating he'd taken. Now, with peace at last settling, his shredded nerves had nothing to focus on saving the pain enveloping him.

"We have to find them horses. So, let's get moving."

Cole, pressing his hand against his forehead, took another glance towards the dead rider, stooped down, picked up the man's revolver and begrudgingly followed Renshaw into the trees.

CHAPTER FIVE

After some hours searching, they came across their horses beside a brook quietly grazing on some patches of lush grass. They appeared unharmed by their ordeal, but not Cole. By now, the beating he had taken previously was beginning to cause him a great deal of discomfort. During the furious firefight, all of his pain had been pushed to the back of his mind, but now, with normality having returned, exhaustion overwhelmed him. Blood seeped from his nose and mouth, and the effort of climbing into the saddle brought such a surge of pain that he almost vomited.

"Boy," said Renshaw, shaking his head and chuckling to himself, "you need to find yourself some more of that sand I thought you possessed. Seems to me that mercy killing has turned you soft."

Leaning across the pommel, Cole shot him a vicious look. "Damn your eyes, Renshaw. That was no mercy killing. That was murder, pure and simple."

"You say any of that back in camp and I'll kill yeh. You understand me, boy?"

If anything, the term 'boy' rankled Cole more than that of 'squirt,' but again, he kept his thoughts to himself. Renshaw was in a dangerous mood. He hoped, as long as he took it easy enough, he could survive until camp. Then, perhaps, he could receive some comfort and care from the army surgeon. He hoped. But, as Renshaw spurred his horse and broke it into a canter, he doubted such a hope would be realised anytime soon. Renshaw cared for one thing and one thing only – himself. Cole mused that there must be a reward on Cairn's head. That would explain the man's almost fanatical desire to see Cairns dead. It was something Cole would need to check when he was well enough. Right now, the most pressing thought was how to ride without pain. He felt sure his ribs were bust. He'd heard from some of the men that often, such an injury led to bleeding inside, and the thought terrified him.

"Boy," came Renshaw's voice as he reined in his horse and twisted in the saddle to study his young companion, "I ain't waiting on yeh. You keep up or I'll leave you behind."

Cole no longer had the strength nor the desire to answer. The last thing he was aware of was Renshaw galloping off, leaving him to fend for himself. With the sun on his back, he clung onto his horse's mane and prayed he would arrive at the camp in one piece.

He remembers cool water splashing across his mouth.

A calm, concerned voice asking him his name.

A woman's voice; later, a man, and hands lifting him. Somehow, he asks them who they are, where he is. The answers are mumbled, nothing definite. He doesn't care. He allows whoever it is to take him to wherever they wish.

There is a face. A big, beefy face, with a grin. Why is he grinning?

"Cole," comes the voice from a hundred miles away, "Cole, you is one tough individual, I'll say that."

It is Burnside. It has to be Burnside, the man who recruited him all that time ago. He tries to concentrate on the memory, to give himself something to hang onto, to recognise. But, then the world recedes once more, and he slips into the soft, welcoming embrace of unconsciousness.

He thinks he smells something medicinal. Clean. Crisp bed sheets. A deep, soft pillow. Someone is bathing his forehead. What is that smell? It is somewhere between sweet and something he used to pick up while sitting beside his mother as she clung to life.

"Reuben? *Cole,* are you there?"

He blinks open his eyes. The kind, anxious face of a man he has never seen before fills his vision. A man dressed in shirt-sleeves, the braces thick on his shoulders, but not as thick as the great handlebar moustache he sports with obvious pride, looks down at him. He smiles and pops a cigar into his mouth. "Well, good morning to you, Reuben. How you feeling?"

"Like I've been hit by a steam locomotive." Cole draped his forearm across his eyes to block out the bright lights of the room. "Where am I?"

"You're back at camp. I don't know how you did it, but you managed to get yourself back here. You're a marvel, young man."

"I don't recollect much, but I reckon it's my horse that should be taking the credit."

"I'm not surprised your memory is all screwed up. You've taken quite a beating, Reuben, and you'll need to rest for a couple of days, but there's nothing life-threatening."

Reuben tried to move, but the pain around his body proved too great. Straining to look, he noticed the bandaging around his chest, so tight he could barely breathe.

"You bust a couple of ribs. Your nose and jaw ain't bust, so you're lucky – you'll keep your good looks!"

He laughed, but Cole could not join in. Instead, he groaned and winced. The more conscious he became, the more discomfort he felt.

He tried his best to sleep.

Throughout the subsequent days, he rested. Around him, the occasional orderly would flit, bringing him soup – his jaw was too swollen for him to chew down solids – and drinks. On the fourth morning, with a good deal of encouragement from the army doctor, he sat up, attended to himself, washed and attempted some tentative stretching exercises.

From the door, a young girl no more than fifteen studied him, an impish grin on her pretty face.

"Penny, you skedaddle," said the doctor, noticing her.

"Ah, Pa, I ain't doing nothing."

"I know, which is why I want you to scoot. Now, go on, get out from here. The poor boy needs to rest."

"He don't look poor from where I'm standing. He looks just fine."

Cole sniggered, "I'm not feeling so fine, miss."

"You can call me Penny. Everyone else does."

With that, the doctor's patience snapped, and he hustled her out of the door and closed it behind her with a resounding crash. "Just like her mother – never does as she's told."

"It's good to see a pretty face, doc."

"Oh? Is that you feeling better?"

"A little. I think. Let me see..." He tried another stretch and winced as a jolt of pain travelled through his body.

"Those ribs will take a while to heal completely," the doctor explained as Cole, taking a few tentative breaths, slowly eased himself out of bed. He waited, preparing himself for another stab of pain, but when none came, he began to move around the cramped room, groping from one piece of furniture to the next for support. He was willing to do whatever it took to return manoeuvrability to his limbs. "You have to be patient, Reuben. You're young and healthy, so you'll mend soon enough. Just don't push yourself too far. You have two cracked ribs. The man who laid into you must have been a pretty mean prize-fighter I would say."

"He is a murdering ..." He swallowed down his words, shook his head, and collapsed onto the edge of his bed.

There came a knock on the door and a young corporal entered, snapping to attention. "Sorry to disturb you, sir, but the Colonel wishes to talk to Cole in his quarters as soon as convenient."

"That's kind of him," muttered the surgeon. "Are you up to walking across to the Colonel's quarters, Reuben?"

"I think so. I'll give it a try anyways."

The doctor beamed. "Good man! Very well, corporal. Kindly inform the colonel that Reuben Cole will attend within the next half hour or so."

The corporal saluted again, twirled on his heels and left. The doctor went to follow him.

"I want to thank you, sir. For everything you've done."

At the door, the doctor smiled, his jawline reddening slightly. "Don't mention it. You're lucky you came in when you did because in a few days, the army will be moving again, and I think there's gonna be some serious fighting with the Rebs. Rumour has it they have a new commander-in-chief, who is not only a tough old coot, but a damned fine soldier. Goes by the name of Lee, or so I understand. He's replacing Johnston, who was wounded at Fair Oakes. Things are going to get mighty hairy, young fella. And, none of it is gonna ease until this whole bloody mess is ended."

They'd built the temporary fort quickly and it showed. Already, the wooden walls were warped, some teetering on collapse. It would take a brave man to climb the roughly hewn ladder to the top of the single lookout tower. Below, on two sides of the parade ground, there were low buildings, verandas held up by wobbly posts, but the most soundly built structure was where the colonel had his quarters. In a room within this, Cole found his commanding officer poring over a large campaign map laid out across his desk. Other officers flanked him. They all looked serious as Cole did his level best to give a salute. He felt decidedly self-conscious in his torn and tattered scouting clothes and his inability to stand ramrod straight. The colonel, however, as he looked up and studied the young scout, did not appear to notice. Instead, he beamed and came around the table, hand thrust out.

"Reuben Cole! Pleased to meet you, young fella!"

He pumped an incredulous Cole's hand.

"Don't look so shocked. What you did over the past few days, son, defies belief! How old are you again?"

Cole had to stop himself from blurting the truth. Instead, he said weakly, "Eighteen, sir."

"Eighteen?" He arched a single eyebrow. "Well, well... Gentlemen, this here is the spirit of our Union. Young men willing to risk their lives in order to keep our glorious country together!"

The other officers chimed in with a collection of congratulations and words of praise. Cole stood there, the heat rising over his face, and longed to turn and run. Instead, he managed to mumble a few thank you's.

"You up to talking, son?"

"I am, sir."

"Good. Danebridge, bring a chair."

One of the officers quickly grabbed a nearby hardback chair and brought it to Cole, who sat down with as much care as he could, wincing as the pain sliced through his ribs.

Eying him with interest, the colonel leaned back on the table and folded his arms. "Cairns ran us a merry dance for well over six months, son. As you know, Major-General McClellan planned to attack and subdue Richmond. After Williamsburg, we attempted an amphibious assault, but it was thwarted. The Rebs seemed to know our every move. Now, they were either extraordinarily lucky, or they had some pre-warning. We now know it was the latter. Cairns was feeding them information. Every step we made was being telegraphed to Johnston and his army. Our man, Lieutenant Renshaw, managed to ingratiate himself into Cairn's trust, and we all know what happened next. You shot him, I understand?"

"Cairns, sir? Yes, I did. In the leg. Unfortunately, he still managed to escape."

"And, you managed that despite having received the beating of your life."

Cole lowered his head, unable to hold the colonel's stare. "Yes, sir."

"I'm writing a letter of commendation to the General for what you did, young man. A citation."

"Oh my..." Cole's heart almost missed a beat. He sat and stared, unable to speak. All he could manage was a pathetic smile and a slight shake of the head. His face was so hot he felt it would erupt into flames.

"Son, you have conducted yourself with extraordinary bravery and it is only right it is officially commended. It's thanks to Renshaw for this as it was he who detailed what happened."

Again, Cole reeled at this disclosure. Renshaw, who he believed would have gladly left him for dead, the one whose constant jibes and criticisms brought Cole to distraction, was responsible for praising Cole to the four winds?

"Thing is, young man," said the colonel, pushing himself off the table, his face now a perfect mask of stone-cold seriousness, "the regiment will be moving out in less than two weeks to rendezvous with the rest of the Army of the Potomac. I can't say too much about what is happening, but intelligence gathering is essential. Coupled with counter-intelligence, of course. We want you to go out there again, find him and nullify his operations."

"Cairns?"

"The very same. I understand you're not feeling up to it right now, but time is against us. So, you and Renshaw will set out again in five more days. My advice, young man, is to get yourself up to a fitness level that will see you in good stead to face the rigours that await."

"Yes, sir," said Cole, automatically. "I will start straight away, get my eye back in." He unconsciously patted his hip where his pistol would usually sit.

"Renshaw tells me you are a first-class tracker. There is no one else of your calibre, young man. That's why I need you – *we* need you. All of us."

"I shall not let you down, sir."

The colonel's smile broadened. "I didn't doubt it, son."

Getting to his feet, Cole saluted stiffly and went outside.

Standing there, leaning against a post, was Renshaw, a wry smile on his face. He was chomping on a wodge of tobacco, a long line of which he spat out as Cole drew closer.

"You up to this, squirt?"

Cole sighed. "You never stop, do you, Renshaw."

"Stop? Stop at what?"

"The chides, the remarks. I ain't no squirt, Renshaw, nor am I your boy. You would have gladly left me for dead out there, probably taking all the glory for yourself."

"You seem to have got that all up on its ass, Cole. It was me who commended your bravery to the colonel."

Cole couldn't help but smile at Renshaw's use of his actual name. A small victory, but a victory nevertheless. "Yeah, the colonel told me that. You only did that because I survived and you were fearful I might report you. You had no choice."

"A bit of gratitude would go a long way, you ignorant cur."

"For what? You leaving me out there to die?"

"If I'd left you, you'd be dead."

"I got here by myself, Renshaw, while you was no doubt lubricating your dry throat over in the mess hall."

"You're talking yourself straight into another beating."

"You think so? We still have unfinished business, you and me. I ain't forgotten what passed between us."

"Me neither."

"Good. Because when this is done, I aim to teach you straight, Renshaw." He tilted his head and held the man's furious glare. "In a fair fight, Renshaw. If you can manage that much."

Renshaw sneered, turned and sauntered away. It gave Cole no pleasure in watching him dip his head as he entered the mess hall, an action that confirmed everything Cole thought of the man.

CHAPTER SIX

He took himself some distance from the camp to an isolated glade, shaded from the noonday sun by the overhanging branches of the encroaching trees. There, in the cool of the dappled greenery, he set up some pieces of wood, measured out twelve paces, and drew his pistol. He carefully eased off single shots from a Colt Patterson he'd borrowed from one of his fellow recruits at the bunkhouse.

Inevitably, as he himself had guessed, the first shots went wide of the mark. After four rounds, he lowered the piece, settled his breathing, and tried again. The fifth shot took out a tiny corner of one of the hunks of wood. With deliberate slowness, he reloaded the five-chambered cylinder. Fortunately, this later model was fitted with a hinged loading lever, so there was no need to disassemble the weapon. It was a fine gun, and as Cole at last aimed down the long barrel again, he grunted with satisfaction as the first bullet slapped dead centre into the piece of wood.

From then on, it was a simple process of aim, squeeze, fire, discharging each slug with unerring accuracy.

He chuckled to himself as he opened up the reloading lever to clean out the gun once more.

"You're what's known as a natural, Mr Cole."

He swung around in some surprise to find Penny, the army doctor's daughter, sitting on an overturned tree trunk, hands curled around a reed basket sitting in her lap. She wore a full, light blue patterned summer frock, with a matching bonnet set jauntily on her head. His tongue grew thick in his mouth as he gazed upon her, unable to speak, heartbeat pounding in his throat.

"Don't look so shocked, Mr Cole," she slipped off the trunk and walked towards him with so much confidence and grace she caused Cole to reel backwards, all thoughts of the gun in his hand forgotten. "I'm sure you've received compliments before, isn't that just so?"

Her smile was warm and friendly, her eyes twinkling with that same impishness he had found so entrancing the first time he'd seen her. Now, with her so close, the smell of her perfume in his nostrils, he could hardly breathe, let alone think. He merely gaped.

"Are you all right, Mr Cole?" She gave a short laugh and looked skywards. "Sure is a beautiful day. Are you going to be practising for all of it?"

He mumbled something incoherent, shaking his head furiously.

"No? Ah, because I was hoping you might accompany me on a short walk down to the river. We could look out for rails or coots. You never know, we might get lucky and spot a kingfisher."

She took his hand. With his eyes on stalks, he watched her fold her fingers around his.

"Shall we?"

Mute, unable to resist, he allowed himself to be guided through the surrounding trees and down a small incline to where a tributary trickled by. Birds sang above the gentle sound of water tumbling over rocks, but Cole heard none of it. His world, together with his perception of it, had been hi-jacked by this girl's loveliness.

They sat, and she watched the river whilst he watched her. Nothing in nature was more beautiful, or so it seemed to Cole at that moment. As he studied her fine profile, with those full lips and cute, snub nose, he, at last, found the courage to speak. "Miss, er, I don't …"

"You can call me Penny, Mr Cole. Pa says your Christian name is Reuben? Is that so?"

He nodded weakly. "Penny. Yes… I, er, Penny… What's a coot?"

She frowned at him. "A coot? You don't know?"

"No. Nor a rail. A kingfisher, I think I have heard of them, but I don't know much about rivers as I was born and raised on a ranch. Horses, now I knows about them! But, not coots."

She laughed. "You're funny, Reuben. A ranch? Well, let me see… A coot, together with a rail, they are birds found near water. They *live* on water. Kingfisher, more accurately, the Belted Kingfisher, now he is what his name implies. He fishes. He waits on an overhanging branch, peering into the waters, waiting for that silvery flash and then" she shot her hand in a downward motion "he dives and strikes. He is a treat to behold, Reuben."

As she spoke, his eyes rested on her mouth, the way her lips formed each word, each syllable, and he was mesmerised. From somewhere, he heard laughter, and he blinked and emerged from his reverie to find her staring, laughing. "Are you listening to me, Reuben Cole?"

He threw up his hands, suddenly terrified that he had offended her. "Yes! Yes, I am, Miss – I mean *Penny*. Of course I'm listening. What you're saying, it's interesting. I know nothing about birds and such."

"So, being with me, Reuben Cole, is something like an education."

He wasn't sure if she was mocking him, so he remained quiet. Despite his heart thundering inside his chest, the swelling in his throat was easing and he was growing more confident. She still terrified him, however, her confidence unnerving him to the very core of his being. Even going up against Cairns and those assorted Reb riders was nothing in comparison to the effect she was having on him!

"I'd like you to come to supper, Reuben." He snapped his head around to her, his mouth yawning open. Again, dumb-struck, he could not say a word. "I've spoken to Papa and he is agreed. He said you are a young man of admirable qualities and excellent spirit. I don't often hear Papa talk like that about anyone. There are so many young men coming through camp now, some of whom appear so young, so innocent, and I am sad to relate, some do not come back after forays with the enemy. You, on the other hand, you are different. Eighteen, but you have the demeanour of someone much older."

"Please, Penny," he said, holding up his hand, "stop. I am not accustomed to praise and it... Well, to be honest—"

"Oh yes, Reuben, *be* honest."

He blinked several times. "Praise... People telling me how well I have done, all of that. It makes me uncomfortable, truth be known."

"That's what's known as modesty, Reuben, and there's nothing to be ashamed of in that. But, you will come to supper – and I promise I will refrain from praising you too highly."

She laughed, waited for him to join in, and laughed even louder and longer after he did so.

"This evening. Seven o'clock," she added when they both finally stopped.

"It'll be my pleasure."

"I know it will."

They laughed again, the sound carrying almost all the way back to the camp.

Across from the dining table, Reuben sat and waited, hands on his lap. He knew enough about etiquette to know it was unseemly to put your elbows on the table. He felt a little like a schoolboy placed under scrutiny by his elders and betters. Dressed in a neat, clean and well-brushed jacket he'd borrowed from another fellow recruit, he did his best to smile and nod graciously whenever Penny's mother loomed over his shoulder to take away his empty plate and serve him another course.

"My, Reuben," said Penny, "you do indeed have a mighty appetite."

He shot a quick glance towards the doctor, sitting at the head of the table in a crisp white shirt, adorned with a bow tie and speckled maroon and black waistcoat. "Nothing wrong in that, Pen," said the doctor.

"No, I did not mean it as a criticism, more of an observation."

"I would suppose that long days in the saddle, eating nothing but hard-tack and biscuits would give a man an appetite for good food. Wouldn't you say so, Reuben?"

"Indeed, I would, sir."

"So, you eat all you want, Reuben," said Penny's mother, returning to the room with a large serving bowl of steaming potatoes. "You want more steak?"

"Oh, no thank you, ma'am," replied Cole between mouthfuls, "this is just fine."

"Well, we have plenty. Here," she ladled potatoes onto his plate and poured thick gravy over them. "We have wine."

"We do?" asked the doctor, staring at her in wide-eyed disbelief. "My, this *is* a feast!"

The evening continued with much laughter, and Cole, relaxing for the first time in many months, found himself slowly revealing more about his life than he had planned. Later, stepping out for a stroll around the doctor's impressive garden, Penny drew him to a swing in the far corner. Settling down, Cole stood and watched. She seemed so happy, so full of life. He envied her and wished he, too, could be so at ease with himself and the world.

"You've seen a lot in your young life, Reuben," she said suddenly.

Her words caught him off guard. He stuck his thumbs in his belt and looked away, awkward, uncomfortable. "I guess."

"What you were saying during dinner, about riding out on the range, about that Indian... what was his name?"

"Brown Bear."

"Strange names they have, don't they. I have recently read Fennimore Cooper's Last of the Mohicans. You have read it?"

"Can't say I have."

"There are many curious names in that book. The villain is a Huron by the name of Magua. It translates as Sly Fox."

"I'm guessing that is probably a name the author gave him. I have only known one native and that is Brown Bear. I do not know how he came by his name."

"A savage, no doubt."

He cocked his head, frowning. "He was perhaps the most honourable and brave man I have ever known. He saved my life."

She looked and sounded shocked when she said, "Lord. Truly?"

"I would not say it if it were not so. Miss Penny, you living here, not far from a soldiers' camp in the most dangerous of times, you should know that this land is filled with all sorts of tales. Most of 'em are untrue. This one, I assure you, is totally genuine."

"You said you saved *his* life. You said nothing about him returning the favour."

"I would not class it as a favour, Penny. It was not planned for, he reacted, as I did, to a grave situation."

"But, to save your life, that is admirable, Reuben. An honourable deed. Like yours."

Feeling the heat rising to his face, he looked away again. "I don't know much about that."

"I'm surprised, though. I have heard men speak of Indians as bloodthirsty. They raid, murder, scalp and many other things far more vile."

"Which we have done to them ever since white people came to this land. That's the truth of it. As for scalping... Well, that is not a traditional act, Penny... not something they did naturally."

"I don't profess to know the whole story, but Fennimore Cooper's novel taught me a lot. This is a brutal land, as you have said, but it is one that is being tamed. I am certain that after this dreadful war is ended, we shall experience a new era of freedom and equality. Don't you?"

"I have no idea. Freedom... Not sure what that is. I have felt *free* when I am out on the range with only myself to tend to. But, I ain't experienced anywhere near enough to pass judgment on such things. I'm barely out of short trousers, Miss Penny. I may look rough and ready, but I ain't, and that's for sure."

"I'm glad of that, Reuben. I would want us to be friends."

"Me, too, Miss Penny. Me, too."

She blew out her cheeks. "Penny, just Penny."

He nodded and smiled.

After returning to the house, Cole thanked the doctor and his wife for allowing him to be their guest. On the main porch, he went to descend the steps to the path leading to the camp, but stopped and turned to face Penny. "Thank you," he said, carefully repositioning his hat. "I had a good time, Penny. I hope to see you soon."

"Oh, Reuben." She came down the steps to him and put her arms around him. "I don't want you to go away. I want you to stay in camp, visit me whenever you can."

He stood treelike, stiff and unbending... her words sending his emotions into confusion. "I don't have much choice, Penny. I have to go out onto the trail again in a few days, find Cairns and—"

"I don't want to know the details," she said sharply, stepping away from him. Her eyes shone with tears. "I just want you to come back safe. You hear me?"

He forced a smile, thinking it the correct response. "I'll do my best, Penny. I promise."

"I want to know everything about you, you hear?"

"Perhaps we could meet again? Say, tomorrow?"

"My, you have become the bold one." Her voice, so light, so natural, sounded full of happiness with a hint of enthusiasm.

Smiling openly, Cole pressed on, "I see you have a little buggy out back."

"Yes. It's mama's. Why do you ask?"

"I thought perhaps I could take you out, on a picnic, if that is not too bold... tomorrow?"

"That would be very nice, Reuben."

"Noon?"

She nodded. "How many days before you leave?"

"Five. But, when I return, we'll have plenty of time to get to know one another a whole lot better."

"You make damned sure you keep that promise of yours, Reuben Cole."

"You shouldn't cuss."

She gasped. "You've heard much worse, I'm sure."

"But, not from someone as pretty as you."

Now it was her turn to blush, and he moved away, a tiny sense of triumph making itself felt in his fluttering stomach. At the gate to the front garden, he turned and waved. She waved back. He could see she was crying, and he thought how cruel life was that he should meet someone so lovely just as he was about to descend once more into the uncertainties of life as a tracker.

It was a thought which he was to keep with him throughout the ensuing days.

CHAPTER SEVEN

He slept well and woke feeling refreshed, the memories of the previous evening giving him a warm feeling inside. He went outside to where a breakfast of sorts was being served up by the cook. Thick ham, more fat than meat, and fried potatoes drenched in grease. The coffee tasted bitter, the bread meant to soak up the fat like a hunk of stone. He left, spirits deflated, and promised himself he would buy some good cuts for the journey. Salted they may be, but anything would be better than the recent concoction he had forced himself to swallow.

He went again to the secluded glade and fired off more rounds, this time, with a good deal more success. The Paterson felt good in his hands, almost as good as his old Remington.

Tramping across the parade ground on his way back to his bunkhouse, he caught sight of several groups of soldiers in shirt-sleeve order loading up bags of grain into waiting wagons. Others were checking rifled-muskets, powder and ball. All looked busy and awash with sweat as they prepared for the next phase of McClellan's plan to strike towards the Confederate capital, Richmond.

"Your name Cole?"

He turned to see a huge hulking brute of a man towering

over him. His shirtsleeves were rolled high up over bulging biceps. Forearms bristling with thickly matted hair led to gnarled hands which, when balled up into fists, were frightening in their size and capability.

Cole couldn't help but swallow hard. "It is. You have me at a disadvantage."

"Name's Arnoldson. The colonel spoke to me about you."

"Oh." Cole looked around. Nobody seemed to be taking any notice of him, and certainly there was no sign of the colonel or any other officer. "So... what is it you want, Mr Arnoldson?"

"Just Arnoldson will do."

"All right. Arnoldson, how can I help?"

"I'm here to help *you*, son." He jabbed a large, meaty finger to an area behind the barracks. "There's an open area of scrub yonder. We'll go there."

The big man took a step, but Cole baulked and held up a hand. "Wait a moment. What for? What is it you want to help me with?"

"These are the colonel's orders, so don't fret none."

"Look, Arnoldson, I'm indebted, but I have no idea what it is you or the colonel wants or—"

"Just get yourself in line with me, son. I'm a sergeant, so you follow my orders." His frown deepened. "And, shut up with the questions."

Leaving Cole in bemusement, the big man strode away. Cole, not knowing what awaited him, touched the butt of the Paterson. If this was some sort of ambush, possibly orchestrated by Renshaw, then he would not hesitate in blasting his way out of it. For now, he'd see what played out, and so, reluctantly, he followed the hulking sergeant hoping somebody would bear witness to any ill-doing.

Nobody did.

Reaching the area, Cole took a moment to scan the surroundings. It was a flat, open, hard piece of earth with no cover for any waiting assailant. Perhaps this wasn't an ambush after all.

The big sergeant stood like an immovable granite pillar, his eyes black, alert, intense. Cole, intimidated and nervous, waited. Arnoldson had ordered him not to speak, and it was clear that this was not a man to argue with.

"Colonel has reports that you fought like a wildcat with Cairns. But, Cairns is tough. He knows how to fight. You, although you're brave enough, have not the skills to overcome someone like him. I'm here to show you how you can."

Blinking, Cole brought up both hands. "That's kind of you, but I ain't got no time to be learning stuff like that. We're leaving in a few days, and there is much to prepare. Anything you can—"

"If you can fight as well as you can talk, then my work here is done. I doubt it, however. So, come on, let's get to it. Move in close, give me your best punch."

Cole did not move. "Mister, this ain't gonna—"

"If I have to tell you anything twice again, I'll break your damned jaw. Now, come on, dance."

It wasn't pretty and it wasn't effective. Cole, feeling his muscles clench with frustration and anger, moved in and swung. He missed. The big man moved with surprising grace, nimble as a ballet dancer. Cole, undeterred and determined to prove his prowess to this bear of a man, slammed in a left, another right. Both blows were blocked with ease. He tried another combination, but only succeeded in hitting thin air.

Cole stood, hands on hips, loudly sucking in his breath. The man was a magician, one moment there as big as a barn door, the next, in a completely new position. Cole blew out a frustrated sigh.

"Move, son," said Arnoldson, his breathing even, body relaxed. His big hands swatted away every attempted punch, and each time, he swayed and bobbed until, at long last, he countered with a flick of his outstretched fingers into Cole's face. The blow, more of a tickle, enraged Cole, forcing him to press harder, swing wider. His breathing grew louder, the sweat dripping into his eyes. The physical exertions coupled with his rising anger were proving a distinct handicap to any successful blow. He gathered himself, determined to land at least one punch, and rushed forward.

The big man stepped away, allowing Cole to come onto him, catching him off balance. Unable to check his forward momentum, Cole stumbled over Arnoldson's outstretched leg and received a powerful cuff on the back of his neck to help him on his way, and he fell face-first into the dusty ground.

He lay there, spent and winded, coughing as flurries of dust invaded his mouth and nostrils. His head rang with the force of Arnoldson's blow and he rolled over, clutching at his neck. He blew out his exasperation. "Damn, how in the Hell am I meant to get anywhere near you?"

Arnoldson stood with fists on hips, grinning. "That's what you're here to learn, son. Now, get up and let's start again."

"I need some water."

"You'll get it when you manage to land a punch." He shook out his hands, bunched his fists again, and went into a half-crouch. "Now, get to it!"

Over the course of three sessions, Cole received not only a sound thrashing, but also an insight into how to check an opponent's attack, how to use their weight and strength against them, deliver crushing blows and some instruction on vulnerable parts of the human body and how to strike them effectively. At the end of it, he sat on the ground, head bowed, sweat dripping from the tip of his nose. Arnoldson stood over him, thrusting a water canteen into his hands. "You've earned that."

"You think so?"

Arnoldson grunted. "Eighteen, the colonel said you were." He turned down the corner of his mouth. "You're not. You lied about your age so you could sign up for the army. Don't tell me I'm wrong. You haven't quite developed your physical strength. You will, but not yet." Cole held his breath, wondering what was coming next. A report to the colonel, perhaps? Arnoldson's eyes narrowed. "What are you, sixteen?"

Without looking away, Cole raised the bottle to his lips and drank. "Uh-huh." He tensed, ready to make a run for it. He had no idea what the punishment could be for falsifying his papers, but he wasn't prepared to hang around and find out.

"If you live, and of that, there is no guarantee," continued Arnoldson, "then I reckon you will come out of this as someone formidable."

"Formidable? I hope so."

"But, you have to practise. Practise and fitness, there is no substitution for those. So, we shall meet, same time every day for the next five days. That's how long you have before you leave, so I understand."

"Every day? But, what about—"

"My orders are to get you up to scratch. Colonel tells me you received a beating, that your ribs were busted. I'll give you some consideration because of that," a thin smile developed across his broad face, "but not much."

"You're so full of kindness, Arnoldson, it almost brings me to tears."

"That supposed to be funny?"

"Nope. Just a jest is all."

"Well, don't. I want you to take this seriously." He pointed to Cole's Paterson. "They say you are good with that. Well, thing is, if you lose it, you need to know how to come out of any scrape alive. You understand?" Cole nodded. "You've got to *want* this, son. The desire. You must *want* to prevail. In any fight, you must be prepared to do whatever it takes. Skill is not enough. It's here," he punched his own chest, "here is where victory lies. Don't forget that, Cole."

"I won't. And, thanks. I'll come along, practise every day, the moves, the exercises you showed me, everything."

"And, the heart."

"Oh yes, I won't forget the heart." He took his time replacing the stopper in the canteen. "So, Mr Arnoldson, me being sixteen ain't gonna hold me back none?"

"Son, I've seen men twice your age who do not have as much sand as you. I reckon you'll do."

The big man threw out his hand. Cole took it and pulled himself to his feet. He smiled into Arnoldson's face. "I'll sleep well tonight."

"Exercise in the morning. Your muscles will feel like rock. You have to loosen them up. After that, we'll meet up and you'll be fine."

"What about my breakfast?"

Arnoldson tilted his head. "You call that swill they serve a breakfast?"

"No, but I'll need something in my—"

"You can take coffee after the session – not before."

They shook hands and Cole wandered off, already experiencing several twinges in muscles he never knew he had.

CHAPTER EIGHT

The next few days fell into a routine of waking, stretching, then shooting. After that, he'd face Arnoldson striving his utmost to land a blow before taking breakfast, sometimes finding it almost impossible to sit down without crying out with the pain of the blows he'd received.

He met Penny at noon of that first day, and they rode out into the surrounding countryside. Penny twirled her parasol and Reuben handled the little buggy with consummate skill. The small, sprightly pony proved strong and game. They both enjoyed the ride more than the picnic, which was a frugal affair.

On the riverbank, Penny threw out a blanket, and they sat and stared at the water without speaking. Cole finding, with some surprise, that he did not feel awkward at all, longed for the moment to last forever. Silence was something he liked, and she, too, whether in deference to his mood or something she felt herself. They fell into deep contemplation.

With the sun high in the sky, they both lay back, eyes closed, and enjoyed the simple pleasure of being alive on such a beautiful day.

The ride home was leisurely, and as Cole returned the buggy to the stable at the back, unhitched the pony and set to rubbing it down, Penny watched him with a smile on her face. "You do that like you were born to it, Reuben."

"It's something I've done most of my life – working with horses, tending to 'em, knowing their ways. Without a horse, I'd be lost, Penny. Incomplete."

"You're quite the philosopher, Reuben."

"Am I?" Grinning, he came towards her, wiping his hands on his trousers. "You are what is called learned."

"I've had schooling if that's what you mean."

"No, it's more than that. You're clever. You know lots."

"Knowing lots doesn't make anyone *clever*, Reuben. You're clever, but you don't spend your time in a book."

From nowhere, he lunged forward and took her around the waist. She giggled and he kissed her. She surrendered, gripping his scalp, and their embrace lingered.

They met a few more times during those days. Each time, their longing for each other grew, and Cole experienced sensations he never thought possible. Despite his body and his pride hurting after each session with Arnoldson, he never complained, and found being in the company of Penny the best balm there was.

On the fourth day, the colonel summoned both him and Renshaw to his office.

The colonel appeared serious, more so than at any other point. He sat behind his desk, chin in hands, peering down at a large map laid out in front of him. "Situation is grave, graver than any of us imagined. The Rebs are putting up stiff resistance, and obviously, they have prior knowledge of our troop movements. Clearly, they have people working within our forces, and it is imperative we weed them out. They are resourceful and we must match them, blow by blow. Therefore, gentlemen, you will leave *today*. Gather your things and set off with all haste. You will be accompanied by one of my chosen men, Thomas Lester. He's an Englishman, known as Red."

"Well, I've known a few redheads," said Renshaw with a low giggle, "and they sure is hotheads!"

The colonel did not appear impressed or amused. "No, Renshaw. He's not a redhead. No doubt he'll explain. He is your superior, Renshaw, a Captain. You understand the significance?"

"Yes, sir. Of course."

"Good. He has sealed orders which he will relay to you as soon as you are well clear of camp."

"All sounds very mysterious, sir."

"You just do as you are told, Renshaw. And Cole," he looked directly towards the young scout, "Arnoldson tells me you have improved beyond all expectation, so I'm pleased to hear that. You know what your task is."

"Yes sir."

"Then, get to it. I want you back here before the regiment moves out. You have one week."

"But, how will we know where to look," put in Renshaw, sounding flustered.

"Captain Lester will guide you, Renshaw, have no fear. Now scoot."

They both saluted and left. Striding across the parade ground towards the main stables, Renshaw rolled himself a cigarette and smoked it feverishly. "Damn it all to hell, I hate working with people I don't know."

"Like me, you mean?"

Renshaw stopped and rounded on his young companion. "It's true you caused me a good deal of trouble, Cole, but I'm over that now. I've learned to live with your arrogance and your petty-mindedness. This new dope, him being a captain an' all, well it don't sit right in my gut."

"The way Cairns did?"

Renshaw's face reddened. "You see, there it is, that clever mouth of yours. Cairns fooled all of us, don't forget. And, don't forget also that you had him in your sights and you missed!"

"I didn't miss. I shot him in the leg, remember."

"Yeah, well if you'd shot him in the right place, none of this would be happening." He threw his finished cigarette away. "What was that the colonel was talking about? About you and someone called Arnson or something."

"Arnoldson. He's a master sergeant. We've been, how shall I put it, swapping notes."

"Notes about what?"

"Life, I suppose you could call it. Yeah... life."

"How old are you again?"

He paused, checking himself unless he revealed the truth. "Eighteen," he said, not daring to match Renshaw's gaze lest he could see the lie burning away there. Eighteen? He wished to God he was eighteen, but that was almost another two years away. Sometimes, he forgot how young he was, and it was only in the dead of night that he remembered, and images of his mother came into his mind, and it was all he could do to bite down the tears. What would she say to him right now if she were still alive, he wondered? He'd seen too much, done too much, and he was scarred by it. All of it. Killing that man who had chased Brown Bear, that was the start of everything. And later, those other killings at the old cabin, how easy they all came to him. If he could change one thing, it would be not to have ridden far away from the ranch that morning. But, he had, and there was no going back, no undoing what he'd done. He'd killed and it had changed him. Changed him forever.

Renshaw fixed him with a scathing look. "I do not believe I spout as much horse shit as you, Cole."

"Then, clearly you haven't been listening to yourself much."

Cole swung away chuckling to himself as the blood boiled red across Renshaw's face.

Later, as they secured bedrolls, blankets, saddlebags and weaponry to their mounts, a man already mounted up approached them. Leaning forward in his saddle, his voice rumbled as if there was sand lodged in his throat. "You be Cole and Renshaw?" he said.

Giving one of the supporting straps a final tug, Renshaw noticed the man and arched an eyebrow. "We are. Who you be?"

The man saluted dismissively with a flick of his hat brim, "I am Captain Lester." His smile was thin, more of leer, bereft of humour. "At your service."

"Good morning, sir," said Cole, returning the salute.

"No need for such formalities," said the Captain, "we'll be riding together for quite a while in terrain we do not know, so it's best if we treat one another as equals."

Renshaw snorted and heaved himself up into his saddle. "Let's get moving, then, Cap'n."

Cole shot him a look, gave a shrug to Lester, and was about to mount up himself when an anxious voice caused him to stop. He turned around and saw Penny running towards him, skirt tails in one hand, the other clamped on top of her bonnet.

"Reuben Cole," she said breathlessly as she reached him. "Were you not going to come and say goodbye?"

With the heat rising, Cole looked across at Lester who did the polite thing and turned away. Renshaw was already walking towards the camp exit.

"I was going to call on you, Penny," he said, which was not a lie. They would pass the doctor's home before they hit the trail proper. "How did you know we was leaving today? We're a day early."

Her eyes twinkled with that mischievousness he found so alluring, "Don't you know anything, Reuben Cole? My papa is the army surgeon. He hears *everything*."

Not sure if that was a good thing or not, Cole took a breath, leaned forward, and kissed her lightly on the cheek. Her eyes widened in shock. "What was that?"

He frowned, but before he could say anything, her arms were around his neck, her lips clamping over his in a long, slow kiss.

There was a low, polite cough, and Cole, prising open one

eye, saw Lester staring with the expression of an annoyed school-master. Slowly, the young scout extricated himself from Penny's embrace. "I'll call on you as soon as I'm back," he said.

"You better, Reuben Cole."

With a glance towards Lester, he climbed into his saddle, waved his hand in a small farewell gesture, and moved away to where Renshaw was already reaching the trail.

He did not look back despite knowing that Penny would be watching him, the tears falling. He could not stand to see that, so he kept his face forward and gave out a silent prayer that the expedition would prove not only successful but quick.

CHAPTER NINE

It was in a small depression enclosed by gorse and small trees that Lester directed them to dismount. Squatting on his haunches, he laid out a rough sketch map, his leather-gloved finger tracing out the direction in which they should follow. "Cairns was last sighted with a detachment of Jeb Stuart's cavalry. Now, we don't know what their overall plan is, but it is safe to assume that Stuart is about to—"

"How you know all this?" interjected Renshaw. He was sat on an outcrop of rock, rolling himself a cigarette. His entire disposition spoke of disinterest verging on contempt for Lester's words.

"We had men in Stuart's camp. He didn't know that, of course, but the information they gave us enabled a detailed—"

"We had men in their camp?"

"As Rebs have men in ours."

A silence spread out between the two men, a dangerous moment charged with tension. Cole, picking up on the icy atmosphere, allowed his hand to fall on his holstered gun.

"How you know *that?*" asked Renshaw, pausing in the process of making his smoke. His eyes bristled with something Cole believed was suspicion, and a touch of accusation, too.

"Why? Does such a revelation come as a surprise?"

"Surprise about what?"

"That we are fully aware of spies in our camp? Renshaw isn't it?"

Renshaw straightened his back. "You know it is."

"You rode with Cairns, a fellow scout. How long were you with him?"

A shrug, the eyes unblinking. "Six months, give or take."

"And, in all that time, you never suspected him?"

"If I had... Listen, *Captain* Lester, I have been in this from the start. First as a scout, but then as an agent of the Federal Government. I was given the task of discovering who the traitor might be."

"Traitor?"

"That's what I said. I linked up with Cairns, not because of any suspicion I had of him, nor anyone else for that matter. It was simply a means of mixing with others, scouts and trackers and the like. People who could almost become invisible. Riding with Cairns, scouting ahead, I never once caught any sign that he might be feeding the enemy information. I was as surprised as anyone when he turned against me and Cole here."

"What about you?" asked Lester, turning to Cole.

"As Renshaw says. I never had any doubt. But then, I hardly knew him, with me being a new recruit an' all."

"So, he was good. Concealing his true colours the way he did."

"Whatever that means," mumbled Renshaw.

"His allegiances," explained Lester with heavy patience. "Nobody suspected he was a secret Reb."

"Maybe," said Cole, "there is more than one. Maybe Cairns was some kind of decoy leading us away from the identity of the real enemy."

"Could be," said Lester slowly. "You shot him, so I understand."

"Not well enough," said Renshaw quickly.

"Well enough to know we'll be looking for a man with a limp."

"I'll know him," said Renshaw. "I'll never forget the bastard, don't worry about that."

"I mean if I'm alone," said Lester.

They all stopped talking, Renshaw taking his time to continue rolling the cigarette, Cole staring at the ground.

"This ain't gonna be easy, boys. We'll be entering a Reb camp. We must remain vigilant. I am the only one Cairns does not know by sight, so it would be best if I were the one who seeks him out."

"But, there could be any number of men with a limp," put in Cole. "We're at war after all."

"True, so I'll nose around. And, I'll do it alone. He'll know you. He'll notice you in a blink and probably blow your head off before you can react."

"So, that's your plan," said Renshaw at last, lighting up his smoke, "to walk into their camp? And, you think they'll just step aside, say 'howdy' and wave you in?"

"I'll be posing as a Confederate officer, Renshaw. I have papers." He patted his breast pocket. None of them wore Union uniforms, having donned an array of civilian clothes.

"You've thought of everything, ain't yeh."

"We'll see," said Lester, and he folded up the map. "Once located, I will apprehend him and hand him over to you. It will be my job to remain in camp and find out what I can about their plans. Jeb Stuart is a remarkable man, courageous and wily, so I'm sure he has his mind well made up as to what he must do. McClellan plans to make an amphibious landing and fall on Richmond. I suspect if Stuart can flank us, he will. All I need to know is in which direction he'll be moving, so our forces can counter."

"Wait," said Renshaw, suddenly alert. "*We* take him in while you stay behind?"

"That's right. I shall enter the camp. You will wait outside and I will bring Cairns to you. Probably at night."

"I don't like the sound of that."

"Oh? And, which part, in particular, do you not like, *Corporal* Renshaw?"

"None of it."

Lester shrugged. "Like it or not, that's what the plan is. Your task is to escort Cairns back to camp where he will stand trial."

"Colonel told me something different," said Cole.

"Situation has changed," said Lester. "He will be interrogated. Anything he can give us as to the identity of the spy in our camp will be worth its weight in gold. So, you keep him *alive,* Cole." His eyes narrowed. "And that is an order."

Cole stiffened. "Yes, sir. Of course."

"Hold on," said Renshaw, puffing out his chest as if he were looking for a fight. "You said we was all equals – none of this officer and men bullshit."

"We are. You can say anything you like, Renshaw, but just so you understand what the hoped-for outcome is."

"His arrest. I got it."

"Good. And now, gentlemen, if I may suggest, we continue on our way. Time is pressing."

———

Several hours later, they made camp. Lester would not allow a fire, so they ate a supper of hard biscuits washed down with water from their canteens. Settling down as night came on, Cole sensed a difference in the air and guessed it meant a change in the weather.

It was sometime close to dawn that the rain came down, forcing them to break camp early and without eating any food. This was something Cole was used to; life on the trail, in the saddle for the most part, missing breakfast, often missing supper, too. The gnawing growling in his guts took most of his attention, the incessant rain the rest. He'd pulled on a cape which was soon drenched and the water, dripping from his hat's rim, splashed onto his mount's mane making the mare no doubt feel as miserable as he did.

Through the cold, hard day, they trundled on, heads down, conversations remaining in their throats. Lester knew where he was going, something which did not sit well with Cole. He shared many of Renshaw's misgivings. However, he did feel some relief in the knowledge that he was not to serve as Cairn's executioner. He'd joined the army as a scout, not an assassin, and as a scout, he wished to remain.

By noon, the rain eased sufficiently enough for Cole to take off his hat and shake it dry. His hair, matted to his forehead, felt dirty as did the rest of his body. Back at the ranch, he'd take a bath almost every day to rid himself of the dust and the sweat from working the horses and the cattle. Out here, the only hope he had of getting washed was a dip in the river, and right now, that was some way off the trail. All around him, the fields spread out lush and green, the rainwater dripping from stems and leaves and branches of the trees. The landscape roundabout was as different from his home as you could possibly get. Softer, rolling, more beautiful. No wonder he'd met Penny in a place like this. Back home, in the harshness of the Territories, the kind of gal he'd have met would have mirrored its hard, unforgiving land.

They rested for a short while, giving them a chance to remove damp clothes and replace them with others from their saddlebags. The land around was too damp to make a fire, even if Lester allowed it, which he didn't. He was keen to press on. They had halted before a slight hillside topped with trees. The sun was forcing the rain clouds away, and the day promised to be better than the previous. Cramming handfuls of biscuits so soggy with the rain that had soaked into the saddlebags, it was as if they were melted. They nevertheless filled a hole. Cole couldn't help but dream of prime beef steaks sizzling on a plate back at the ranch.

All such thoughts left him when the woman came into view.

Dressed in a flowing white dress, she appeared over the crest of the hill, bounding across the fields, her bare legs eating up the distance with all the grace of a deer. Her face, however, was anything but graceful. Two long streams of blood rolled down from her eyes and covered her cheeks. Drawing closer, she spotted the three men for the first time and veered towards them. Open-mouthed, she squawked as if in pain, screeching, "Help! Help!"

Cole was the first to drop from his saddle and move to her.

"Easy," snapped Lester, his gun already in his hand. "Renshaw, take the rise and see if you can see anything."

Renshaw groaned, kicked his horse and urged it up the hill.

Meanwhile, Cole was making a grab for the woman. This close, he could clearly see the state she was in. There were cuts and bruises on her face, the blood crusted over the skin. Dress ripped open, breasts exposed, hair a tangled mess, plastered with sweat... it was obvious to him she had been attacked. As he took her around the waist, she fought back, a wildcat, arms and legs thrashing as he held on. "I'll not," she cried, "I'll not!"

The force of her fight sent them both crashing to the ground. Cole held on, doing his best to calm her. "It's all right," he was saying, pinning her arms. "You're safe, I ain't gonna hurt yeh."

Coming up close, Lester eased himself down from his horse. "Calm down, lady," he said, the gun big in his hand.

Eyes falling on the gun, her face went white. Desperate now, she managed to extricate herself from Cole's hold and scooted backwards, holding out her palms as if this was a hold-up.

"Lady," said Lester, his voice developing an edge, "you need to be still now."

"Please," she said, her voice breaking. "No more. Please."

"Miss," said Cole, propping himself up on his knees, "it's all right now. We're here to help." He shot a worried glance at Lester. "Put the gun away, Captain."

Lester seemed in two minds. He looked away, turning to where Renshaw was making the rise.

"Captain," said Cole again. "Put the gun away, it's frightening her."

At last, Lester did so.

The girl grew visibly calmer.

Smiling, Cole stood up and held out his hand. "Come on, it's gonna be all right."

But, it never was going to be all right.

Renshaw was back with them, and he was breathing hard.

"What is it?"

Renshaw, shaking his head, took a large gulp of water from his canteen before he got the words out. "There's a church and a house. It's burning. And, there's men. A lot of men. Reb cavalry they look like."

"How many, damn your eyes."

He shrugged, looking askance at the girl. "Ten. Maybe twelve. Difficult to make out. They have people on the ground, Cap'n., Women, children."

"Are they your people?" asked Cole quietly, looking at the girl hopefully.

Her wide eyes turned to him. Her lips were trembling, and it was all she could to nod.

"All right," said Lester, as if making a decision. "We move around 'em in a wide arc. It'll only be a small detour, so it won't mean we will—"

"What the hell?" said Renshaw in disbelief. "We can't *leave* those people like that, Cap'n. I saw what they were doing. The women, they were being stripped and... goddamn it, we have to help 'em."

"We can't," said Lester, his eyes locked on the woman. She was sitting up, sobbing. Cole moved close and knelt beside her, putting his arms around her shoulders. This time, she did not fight him off.

"We have to," said Renshaw through gritted teeth. "We can skirt around and take 'em from the flank. They won't know what hit 'em."

"Twelve men, you said. How can we—"

"'Cause they're too busy fucking raping the women, that's why, damn your eyes!"

Lester's eyes flared, but only briefly. "We haven't the time. We need to get to their main camp, find Cairns."

"What if Cairns is with 'em?" said Cole, his words taking the others by surprise. "We should check."

"Did you see Cairns?"

Renshaw screwed up his face. "Jeez, how could I? But, Cole's right. Cairns could be with 'em. They're a scouting party, rooting out supplies no doubt. Scavenging. As a tracker, Cairns could be leading 'em."

Deep in thought, Lester chewed at his bottom lip, unsure what to do.

"Damn you," said Renshaw, turning his horse away, "I'll do it myself."

"Don't be so damned stupid," said Lester. He gestured towards Cole and the woman. "She'll have to stay here. We need you, Cole. If they are twelve, we won't..."

Cole nodded and slowly stood up. "It'll be fine," he said to the woman. "Listen, we have blankets and water. You can sit down underneath a tree and wait for us. We won't be long."

"Cole—"

"Give me a minute, can't you!"

The other two sucked in loud breaths at the ferocity of the young scout's words.

Ignoring them, Cole helped the woman to where a tree stood. It was warm there. "Fetch some blankets," he said, and Lester did so without argument. They lay one on the grass, and after Cole lowered her gently upon it, he draped another around her shoulders. He pressed his canteen into her hands. "Try and rest here," he said, and returned to his horse.

Without a word from anyone, they set off, skirting around the base of the hillside in order to stay out of sight of the men on the other side.

CHAPTER TEN

They lay sprawled in the grass, Lester with a telescope pressed to one eye studying the ensuing horror being played out beside the white, clapboard church some one hundred paces or so away. What remained of a house, or more accurately, a shack burned relentlessly.

Lester had with him the Sharps rifle he so lovingly cleaned each morning. Cole had looked on, fascinated by the man's fastidiousness. Now, he watched as Lester put the telescope aside and squinted down the barrel.

"As soon as I fire," he said calmly, "you two ride down there, guns blazing. It doesn't matter who you hit, if anyone. You'll spook them enough to force them to break."

"And, if we see Cairns?"

Lester turned and studied Cole, his frown deep. "What do you think, Private Cole?"

Cole shrugged, "Shoot him. Not kill him, just wing him in order to put him on the ground."

Lester smiled. "Mount up, boys. It's time to start the party."

Cole moved immediately, but Renshaw hanged back for a moment. "This is a dangerous play."

"That it is, but now that we're here, I cannot allow those

women to be violated the way they are. It is not what I consider war to be."

"I see."

"Do you? You said as much before."

"I still believe we should help. I want those so-called men in the ground."

"We do this right, Renshaw, the way I've ordered."

"I hear you."

"Then, get on your damned horse and wait for the signal."

Cole was checking his Paterson when Renshaw came ambling towards him. Without a word, he delved into one of his saddle-bags and brought out a brace of Colt Navies. He now had three handguns. He handed one of the Navies to Cole. "Best if we have two. We need to fire off as many rounds as we can."

"Are you all right with this, Renshaw?"

"Not much I can do about it." He sighed. "I want those murderous curs put in the ground, Cole, but I don't like the idea of Lester hanging back with that big buffalo gun pointing directly at us."

"You don't trust him?"

Renshaw sighed, his fingers curling around the pommel of his saddle. "There's something... I don't know, Cole. He says he is concerned for the women, but I think it's more that he wants Cairns. But, not for the reasons he says. I don't know... the whole thing... us being out here was supposed to be all about finding what Jeb Stuart's plans are. Colonel seemed mite concerned about that back at the fort. Now, it has all shifted."

"Colonel told me to kill Cairns."

Renshaw seemed about to faint. "He told you – *ordered* you?"

Cole nodded.

"Damn, I ain't never heard of anything like that... Kill Cairns?" Shaking his head, he hauled himself into the saddle, patting the horse's mane to steady it.

Saddling up alongside, Cole put the Navy in his waistband. "Let's get this done, Renshaw. We can unpick it after we have Cairns."

"If we ever get him."

"We will. I think Lester saw him through that telescope of his."

"Damn, Cole, why the hell didn't you say somethin'?"

"Like what?"

Squeezing his lips tight together, Renshaw looked over to his left. "Damn..."

The single gunshot caused them all to startle – men and horses. Renshaw whooped loudly, thrashed away with his reins, and broke his horse into a gallop, Cole only paces behind.

They came around the hillside as fast as their mounts would take them just as a second shot rang out. Renshaw was ahead, yelping like a Reb, Navy in hand. Cole, keeping himself low, picked out the panic ahead. He saw one of the Rebs on the ground, another on his knees holding his stomach, which blossomed red. Men were sprinting, women screaming. A child no more than five was running wild, arms above its head. A little girl, long blonde braids trailing behind her as she ran. She was crying, screaming. Cole couldn't take his eyes off her. He saw a Reb bringing up a gun and Cole fired again, and again. He wasn't sure if any of his bullets hit the man, but it certainly stopped him from taking his shot. He turned wild-eyed and Renshaw opened up, rapid-fire as all hell let loose.

It seemed they were in the midst of a small army as they pulled up their horses, which reared and bucked, whinnying in terror. There were men in various stages of undress, some armed, some not. They were darting each and every way. Women, several on the ground, were struggling to their feet. A man, not a soldier, a preacher dressed all in black, with blood pouring from underneath his high-crowned hat, had his hands clasped in prayer, head turned to the sky. A Reb with a sword lopped off his head with such ease it looked almost like it was choreographed. Cole, dropping to the ground, shot the man, knowing it was too late for the preacher but deriving a good deal of satisfaction at seeing the man fall.

Lester, dismounted and well camouflaged in the tall grass, continued to fire, which put so much confusion into the Rebs they didn't know which way to move. It must have seemed that no matter which direction they turned, an enemy shooter was firing at them.

Slowly recovering, the remaining Rebs were either seeking cover around the church or fumbling for their weapons. Renshaw, who must have been close to being empty, shot two of them. He grabbed for his horse and remounted as several bullets streaked next to him. Cole chanced a look, saw him reaching for the Spencer in its sheath. His pistols were spent, but he made good use of the carbine. Bringing it up to his eyes, despite the horse moving, skittish and afraid, he managed to keep up a good rate of fire while Cole exchanged the Paterson for the Navy Colt.

A Reb came from nowhere, screaming like some hysterical madman, mouth frothing. He had a large, heavy-bladed Bowie knife in his hand and he was charging directly towards Cole. Without a moment's pause, Cole brought up the Navy and fired.

The hammer fell on an empty chamber. Cursing, Cole tried again and again with the same result.

The gun was empty.

Renshaw had given him an empty revolver.

The man was almost on him before Cole moved and clubbed him across the side of the head with the Navy. Stumbling, the man swung, teeth gnashing, striking the knife from side to side. Backing off, Cole threw away the Navy and brought up the Paterson. A single shot hit the man in the chest, the blood erupting before the sound echoed around the verdant fields.

Gaping, Cole peered towards where he believed Lester to be,

and raised his fingers to the brim of his hat and gave a brief grin of thanks. In the ensuing mayhem, he grabbed one of the dead Reb-s pistols and found it had three loaded chambers. Knowing this wasn't enough, he took to loading the others as he looked feverishly around, half expecting to see more Rebs racing to attack him. Any survivors, he soon realised, had made it to the church.

He turned to berate Renshaw for giving him an empty pistol, but there was no sign of him. Within the swirls of drifting smoke, Cole made out Renshaw's horse standing rock still, but of the man, there was nothing but the empty saddle.

Someone grabbed at his ankle and he leapt back, aiming his pistol. He gasped at what he saw. A woman, badly beaten, nose and mouth seeping blood, dishevelled hair, one hand stretched out, imploring him.

Stooping down, he took hold of her shoulders. "It's all right," he said. These were the words he'd uttered to the first woman, the one he'd helped, or tried to. Whoever these men were, soldiers or raiders, Cole no longer considered them human beings. Desperate they may have been, starving even, but to do this...

She fell into his arms and he held her, all the while watching the entrance to the church. He heard the rider coming up behind him, and knew who it was.

Lester dropped from the saddle and stood a few feet away, his breathing hissing through his teeth. "How many are alive?"

"Women?" Cole shrugged, holding the shaking woman closer. "All I do know is there are at least five dead Rebs here. Thanks for saving me."

"I saw you hesitate. That's not good, Cole."

"Cap'n..." He shook his head and buried his face into the top of the woman's head.

"Well, we've got to end this. Where's Renshaw?"

Cole sniffed, sucked in a breath. "I don't know." Lester

frowned, the question frozen on his lips. Cole shrugged. "He gave me an empty pistol. Why would he do that?"

Lester didn't reply. Instead, after a quick glance at the woman, he said, "You wait here, cover the church's main door. I'm going in through the back."

He put down his rifle, drew his two pistols and scurried off towards the rear of the church, smoke enveloping him, turning him into nothing more than a phantom.

Slowly, Cole disentangled himself from the woman and lifted the rifle. It was heavier than he imagined. Looking around, he realised with a degree of alarm that there was little cover anywhere within easy reach. If anyone came out of the church with guns blazing, he'd have little choice but to blow them apart. The thought caused his stomach to flip. None of this was what he wanted. Scouting and tracking... no one ever mentioned anything about ceaseless killing. He wasn't naïve, and he had no misconceptions about what fighting a war could mean, but he never assumed he'd be on the frontline. He should have refused the Colonel's order. He should never have joined up.

"Thank you," came a feeble voice behind him.

He studied her. In another life, he'd find her pretty. "Make your way towards the hillside. There's cover there, and one of your friends is waiting."

"But, what about the others?"

Cole surveyed the scene. The smoke was gradually fading as the house crumbled, sending up bursts of glowing embers. The scene slowly came into focus. Women pulling their garments closer across their bodies, one or two helping others, a mother cradling her baby. The constant drone of sobbing.

"Where are your men?"

"They shot them. Took 'em out back and shot each one in turn. They forced us to watch."

"Dear God."

"I'll tell the others to move away."

In a sudden break in the drifting smoke, he spotted Lester

disappearing behind the back of the church. "Do it quick. There's not much time before it all starts again."

"I will. But, what about you? You can't stay out here in the open."

"I'll be fine." Cole's eyes fell on the Reb who'd charged him, the one Lester had killed with a single shot. He knew there was only one thing to do. "Get moving," he said sharply, and crept over to the dead Reb and lay down, using the body as cover. The close proximity of the corpse brought bile up into his throat, but there was nowhere else to hide, nothing to do but lie and wait. He positioned his neckerchief over his mouth and nose, and did his best not to think of the horror of his situation. He realised, however, that he could not remain like this for long. The most dreadful feeling rose from deep within him, that the body would suddenly sit up and turn its dead face towards him and grin. The thought made him shudder, and again, he had to battle to keep himself from vomiting. To keep himself occupied, he took to reloading both the Paterson and the gun he'd taken from the dead Reb. He worked methodically until both were fully primed.

He concentrated on the entrance to the church, lining up his pistols and the Sharps, his breathing slowly becoming light and easy. He was barely aware of the women moving behind him, their shadows falling over him. He sensed rather than saw them moving away, shuffling towards the hillside, and he found comfort in the fact that they would be safe.

At least for the time being.

CHAPTER ELEVEN

Renshaw had his back to him. Several Rebs were creeping past, making their way across the open ground to where their horses were saddled under the hanging branches of a cluster of trees. All around were the bodies of men, civilians, sprawled out in the dirt, each with a gunshot wound in the head... executions.

Waiting, Lester brought up his pistols and eased back the hammers.

Renshaw swung around, his eyes alive with alarm.

"Wait, Cap'n," he said quickly.

"Traitor is the word you used," he said, "and traitor is what you are."

"No, it's not—"

Lester squeezed both triggers, one after the other, the heavy calibre bullets smashing into Renshaw's chest, throwing him backwards. He was dead before he hit the ground.

Rolling forward, Lester brought his pistols to bear on the Rebs spilling from the rear entrance, racing towards their horses. Knowing they would soon be out of range, he scooped up Renshaw's Spencer and shot them, one after the other, working the lever without thinking about it. Automatic. Ruthless. Efficient. He fired until the rifle was empty.

Casting it aside, he readied his pistols again and bounded into the church.

He gasped.

Cairns was there with a woman locked in his arms. He had a revolver pressed to her head, and her eyes, so full of terror, bored into Lester, pleading with him to help her.

"I'm going to move out of here," said Cairns through gritted teeth. "You make a move against me, whoever you are, and I'll shoot her dead. Now, drop your guns and move away."

Without a moment's thought, Lester did as he was bid. His arms came up automatically in a gesture of surrender.

Cairns slowly moved backwards, the woman sobbing in his grip, and he was grinning.

Cole sucked in his breath as Cairns emerged from the church interior. Submissive, shoulders drooping in silent acceptance of her fate, the girl in his arms wept uncontrollably. The distance between them was less than thirty paces, and Cole could clearly see that Cairns had yet to draw back the hammer of his revolver. He fired a single shot.

After they'd dressed his wound, they lifted Cairns into the saddle, ignoring his cries of pain, and lashed his wrists to the pommel. Due to his constant bleating, Cole wrapped a neckerchief over his mouth and secured it with a harsh pull. "If you need to drink," said the young scout, "just grunt, otherwise keep your mouth shut."

Cole went to his horse, drank from his canteen that was strung there, and pressed his forehead against the horse's rump. Lester had raced down the steps after the shot was fired, a look of confused horror on his face. When he saw Cairns squirming on the ground and the girl safe, he relaxed, saw Cole and smiled.

He told Cole of Renshaw's death, omitting none of the details.

"No one will know it was you," said Cole, holding the man's stare. "He was killed in the crossfire."

Lester nodded and said nothing as he reloaded his weapons. "I'm going to the camp," he said. "As we planned."

"But, we have Cairns now," said Cole urgently. The idea of Lester continuing with the mission seemed absurd to him. "We can get all the information we need from him."

"He won't say anything," said Lester. "Best if I nose around, pick up what I can. We need the direction of Stuart's move towards our forces. Once I have that, I'll return."

"You better, Cap'n. I owe you."

Lester smiled. "That works both ways, private. You've proved yourself today. That shot you made at Cairns, that was something."

"Nah, like fishing in a bucket, Cap'n, I promise you."

They embraced, Lester slapping Cole's back several times. "You'll be fine, with the women and all?"

"We'll be fine, yes. They said there is a town not two miles from here where they are known. I'll escort them that far, then veer back to camp with this piece of filth." He nudged Cairn's leg with a rigid finger. Cairns groaned and glared at him from above the neckerchief mask.

"You watch him. He's as oily as an eel."

"Oh, he won't be no trouble, Cap'n. Have no worries."

"I have no worries about anything to do with you, Cole."

He gave a final nod before turning on his heels.

"Cap'n," shouted Cole.

Lester turned, raising a single eyebrow.

"You never did tell me why they call you Red."

The Captain's grin boarded. "You know anything about England, Cole?"

"Not a thing. I'm not even sure I know where it is!"

"Well, you know I'm English, right?" Cole nodded. "We love cheese over there. There is a county called Leicester, and they make cheese – and it is traditionally red. Has been coloured red for over two hundred years to distinguish it from other cheeses. Red Leicester. Hence, I'm known as *Red,* so christened by some of the Scots in my regiment who picked up on my name." He laughed out loud. "Stupid thing is, I *hate* cheese of any kind!"

Still chuckling to himself, he turned away and tramped back to where his horse was waiting.

Cole watched his back and wondered if he would ever see the man again.

CHAPTER TWELVE

They came at last to another rise, and from there, Cole saw in the depression a small town. It wasn't much, a collection of several clapboard buildings, some more not yet fully erected, clinging to a single tracked street. A church lay at the far end, the most impressive of all the buildings. The women pleaded with Cole to go with them into the town, but he refused, explaining that time was against him and Cairns had to face justice. At this, Cairns muttered a string of obscenities, forcing Cole to rap him around the back of the head with the butt of his revolver.

There was much hugging and tears when Cole finally departed, giving the group a final wave before he disappeared amongst the trees in the general direction of the Union fort he and the others had left days before.

Without speaking, Cole led Cairns, slumped and moaning on the back of his horse, through a landscape punctuated with trees and thickets, lush grass and undulating hills. This was a pleasant land, and in another life, he mused, it would be a good place to settle. His thoughts turned to the afternoon he'd spent with Penny and the regret loomed huge in his mind. He knew exactly what he would do as soon as he got back to camp and the thought brought a smile to his face.

They camped by a river, which gently gurgled its way down towards the distant sea. Cole laid out his bedroll and made a small fire. The weather was chill, and there was little to eat. Cairns, sullen, nibbled on the hard-tack Cole offered him. "This ain't near enough, you idiot."

"Just keep talking, Cairns, and I'll give you another taste of my pistol."

"You're all tough and hardy now, ain't you, Cole. You wouldn't be spouting off so if we were standing toe-to-toe."

Knowing this was a ruse to set him free, Cole ignored the man's jibes. Instead, he walked over to him, lashed his wrists together and secured him to a nearby tree, allowing him enough slack to lie down comfortably. He then relieved Cairns of his boots and returned to his own place. He sat for a long time, staring into nothingness as the evening slowly gave way to night and the fire died into nothing but tiny, spluttering embers.

He awoke early, with the dawn nothing more than a smudged pencil mark across the horizon. After checking Cairns, he wandered off, cutting a path through the trees towards the banks of the river. There, he went through his exercises, limbering up, callisthenics and shadow boxing before stripping off his clothes and plunging into the river to cool his burning muscles. After-wards, he sat, his mind going over all that had happened over the previous days. His eyes glazed over and, without any conscious thought or action, he cried. All of it rose unchecked from the very pit of his soul... the fears, anxieties, the fragility of his youth, Penny. So many regrets, so many actions he wished he'd never allowed. He wept for himself, for what his life had become, for the memories of his mother and how she would be so disappointed if she could see him... and who was to say she could not? He often felt her presence, her silent judgment on the way his life had gone astray, haunting him at every step. She loved him, he knew that much, and he had let her down.

Giving his face another wash, he dried himself off and returned to the makeshift camp to find Cairns struggling against his bindings, face scarlet with the effort. Ignoring him and the many expletives issuing from his mouth, Cole made a small fire and brewed up coffee. They drank in silence before breaking camp and setting off again at their usual, wearisome pace. The land was forgiving, the temperature mild, there was nothing to hold them up or divert them from their course.

Until they came upon the village.

To be more accurate, it was nothing more than a selection of mud huts of various sizes arranged in a haphazard semi-circle. Cole had not seen their like before, and he pulled up his horse and peered upon them with keen interest. Next to him, Cairns snorted. "Probably Shawnee or some such ramshackle tribe that managed to sneak out of a reservation. It happens all the time."

"Shawnee?"

"Maybe, or one of the other Rappahannocks. Who knows, who cares? They're harmless enough."

As they watched, several warriors mounted their ponies and kicked their mounts towards the two scouts. Cole tensed. "You're certain they are harmless?"

"I reckon. Why not give me a gun, then, at least we'll have good odds if anything does go amiss?"

Turning to him, Cole gave him a caustic look. "I don't think so, Cairns."

Cairns shrugged and gave a tiny snigger. "Suit yourself. To me, they're all damn savages, so as they're relieving you of your scalp, I'll simply sit back and enjoy the show."

"You're full of good humour and concern, ain't you, Cairns."

"I do my best to please, squirt."

Cole was about to reply when the warriors rode up, reining in their ponies some ten or so paces from them. They sat and stared.

"Good conversationalists, the Shawnee," said Cairns.

"Shut up, Cairns." Cole studied the four men in front of him.

71

None of the men, half naked, limbs shining with oil, hair hanging limp to their shoulders, spoke. They sat on their ponies, and both animal and man were thin, emaciated almost, with ribs clearly visible beneath their skin... so thin it was almost transparent. They were starving and their eyes, wide and hopeful, seemed to be screaming out for help.

The lead warrior studied the two scouts for some time, inquiring eyes settling on the ropes binding Cairn's wrists together.

"You speak English?" asked Cole at last. He did not fear these men. They did not possess guns. Two had bows, but these were almost certainly reserved for hunting. Some were huddled within themselves, old before their time. They were suffering, all of them, and Cole's primary emotion was one of pity.

"A little," said the man at the front. His gaze shifted from Cairns to Cole. "You are a lawman?"

"We are returning to our camp," explained Cole, speaking slowly. "This here is my prisoner."

Cairns scoffed, "Don't listen to him." He twisted in his saddle. "Shoot these inbreeds, Cole, before they shoot us."

The warriors bristled, exchanging comments in their own tongue with one another. Even without knowing their words, Cole could sense their unease. Cairn's attitude spooked them. Cole was about to try his best to defuse what could be a dangerous situation, but the lead warrior got there first. He held up his hand and answered his comrades with a few, guttural comments before returning to Cole. "We have rabbit. Will you come with us?"

Cairns leaned over his horse and spat into the ground. "Leave me here, squirt. I'll not dine with savages."

"And yet, yourself is one," came back Cole as quick as anything.

The two men glared at one another.

"If you weren't holding all the aces right now, squirt, I'd whup your ass."

A thin smile spread across Cole's mouth. "Oh, I think we can find a way for you to try just that, Cairns."

"You're full of hog's swill. Always was. I whupped you last time and you repaid me by shooting me in the leg. This time, you winged my shoulder, but it won't change nothin'. I'll beat you until you is dead, squirt, despite this damned leg and this cramped up shoulder, so I'd be mite careful about making any such arrangements."

Expelling air loudly through his nose, Cole nodded towards the lead warrior. "I would be honoured, but this one here will be enjoying his own company."

The warrior grunted, turned, and spoke to his comrades. They swiftly swarmed around a bleating Cairns and led him away to a small copse. Cairns did his best to fight them off, but it was hopeless. With little difficulty, before long they had him expertly trussed up to a tree.

Laughing amongst themselves, they made their way towards the camp, Cole turning to see Cairns struggling against the ropes, face red with the exertion, and no doubt, a lot of anger. He couldn't help but derive a good deal of satisfaction at the man's distress.

The meal was a simple one, and Cole, listening to the lead Indian's broken language, gleaned a fair bit from the conversation. As several small children climbed over him, Cole learned that the family group had indeed broken free of their reservation and struck out on their own. They had come across this ancient camp and made it a sort of temporary home, repairing the huts as best they could. There was game in the surrounding fields and forests, but barely enough to sustain them. Fortunately, they had fresh water from the nearby river. The simplicity of their life filled Cole with envy, however, their constant struggle to find enough food made him realise just how precarious their situation was.

"The other," said the lead warrior, "he is a bad man?"

Cole stopped himself from replying at once. Cairns was not wholly bad. No doubt he believed in the Confederate cause, but his traitorous actions left Cole with a nasty taste in his mouth. "He is... misguided."

The warrior frowned. "I do not understand this word."

"It means... His thoughts, his actions, they are not what they should be. He broke our laws and has killed some of my people. I take him back to face justice."

Nodding, the warrior gnawed away at a leg bone before tossing it into the fire around which they sat. "Your people, they wish to do the same with us?"

"Yes. But, you have not murdered." He allowed his gaze to run across the other men. There were six of them in all, and this close up, they did not appear quite as fierce as he had once supposed. They were thin, faces gaunt, eyes black-rimmed. The children who rolled around playfighting and giggling seemed the least affected by their difficult situation. It was clear that the food they managed to catch was given to the young ones first. "At least, I don't think you have."

The lead warrior chuckled. "No. We have not. Life in the reservation, it was more like a prison. Rules. Men made to feel *less* than men."

"And, whisky," put in one of the others. "They gave us much whisky."

Cole arched a single eyebrow. So, some of the others could speak English. How much did they truly understand, he wondered.

They continued to talk for a couple more hours before Cole made his excuses, thanking them for their hospitality. Taking the lead warrior's hand and pumping it with gratitude, Cole felt a lot better than he had before coming across these folk. "I wish you every happiness."

The lead warrior gave him a rueful smile. "That depends, my friend." He walked him away from the camp after Cole bade his farewells, especially to the children, some of whom were already crying at his departure.

At the rise, the Indian waved his hand across the open view. "This land, it is big enough for us all, I think. Yet, your people, you want everything. When you pass this way again, you may not find us here."

"I hope you're wrong. I would like to bring you food and supplies – blankets, ironware, corn."

"You are kind, my friend. For one so young, you speak with much wisdom and understanding."

Feeling the heat rise to his face, Cole looked away. "Maybe. The world is a crazy place right now, and war is a terrible thing. Many will die before it is over, and many of those will be young. Like me. Our youth is already lost to the violence and selfishness of others."

They shook one another's hands again, and Cole, head down, lost in thought, tramped slowly back to where Cairns was waiting, as sullen and as dismissive as he ever was.

CHAPTER THIRTEEN

O n the face of it, little had changed in the fort as Cole rode in the following morning. The place continued to buzz with activity, so much so that nobody paid any attention to the filthy, tired-looking young man leading a sullen, round-shouldered ruffian slumped across a bedraggled mare. Without an exchange of words or looks, Cole dismounted and tied the reins of both horses at a hitching rail, and stretched out his back. He stood on the steps of the commanding officer's quarters and nodded to the burly looking guard on sentry duty. "Is the Colonel inside?"

The sentry studied Cole with a withering look. "Who wants to know?"

"Name's Cole. I was ordered to bring in this prisoner." Cole gestured towards Cairns. "And, here he is."

Grunting a reply, the sentry turned, rapped on the door and went inside. He emerged a few moments later with Lieutenant Danebridge squeezing past him.

"Cole? My God, you've got him!"

Face alight, the Lieutenant came bounding down the steps, gripped Cole by the shoulders, then turned and glared towards

Cairns. "You'll hang, Cairns, for what you've done. Hope you realise that."

Without bothering to acknowledge the officer, Cairns merely repositioned himself in his saddle and released a loud blast of wind.

"He always was an insolent fellow," said the lieutenant, turning up his nose and nodding to the sentry. "Get some more men and escort this prisoner to the brig." He smiled. "Excuse my slip, Cole, but I was a navy man before signing up for the Army of the Potomac as soon as hostilities commenced. I meant jail."

The sentry saluted smartly and scurried off to carry out the young officer's order.

Danebridge took Cole to one side. "The Colonel has travelled across to Camp Nelson to discuss the latest plans with the General. He'll be away for a week or so. On his return, I am expecting our force to march west and engage the enemy."

Still within earshot, Cairns sniggered at this, shook his head, turned away and spat into the ground.

Danebridge glared at the man's back. "No doubt your report will make interesting reading, Cole. You can write, I take it?"

Cole bristled a little. "I can, sir."

"Good. Ah, here's Fowles and the others."

The sentry appeared with three other soldiers, as burly as he was.

"Secure him well, Fowles. I don't want him to have any opportunity to escape."

The soldiers immediately set about dragging Cairns from his horse to escort him across the open space of the camp parade ground to a row of low-level buildings on the opposite side. These were flimsy-looking structures with bowed roofs, cracked adobe walls, tiny windows and rickety doors. As with everything else in the camp, they appeared temporary. They did not instil within Cole any great confidence.

"Are you sure that's a strong enough jail to keep him in?"

The lieutenant fixed Cole with a steely stare. "He'll be in

there for a day at most, so nothing to worry about there. His trial, with your evidence, Cole, will be a formality. I imagine he'll hang the day after tomorrow."

"Well, as long as you are sure, sir, I'll get back to my bunk and start in on that very same report." He brought his heels together and saluted. Danebridge returned it and went back to the confines of the colonel's quarters.

That evening, Cole called on Penny, but there was no answer at her door. Returning to the camp, he inquired of her whereabouts and was told by the quartermaster sergeant that her father, the 'good doctor' had left for an undisclosed location some days previously. The only details he could furnish was that Penny had taken ill.

Cole felt his legs give way under him, forcing him to hold onto the counter which separated him from the quartermaster. "Ill?"

"That's all I know, young fella. Could be you could call in on Mrs Randall over at the officers' quarters. I know she was a good friend of the doc. She might know a little more than me. Sorry."

Reeling away, Cole stood in the open doorway and mopped his brow with his neckerchief.

"Are you all right, young fella?"

Cole didn't respond. He didn't want to. Seized by a crushing feeling of dread, he went out into the evening and slowly made his way to where he hoped to find Mrs Randall.

He could barely contain his relief when she opened the door to her apartment and gave the young scout a polite, yet curious look.

"Mrs Randall? Apologies, ma'am," he hastily pulled off his hat and clutched it between both his hands. "I was told you might know the whereabouts of the good doctor and his daughter, Penny? I am inquiring due to me being—"

"You'll be Reuben," she said softly.

He stopped. Her eyes were already watering and a terrible premonition of dread news bore down upon him. He stuttered, "Y-yes, I am."

"You'd best come in."

The apartment was small and sparsely furnished, with a single main room and bedroom leading off. As with all the buildings in the camp fort, the walls were temporary and flimsy. They shook as Cole wandered past and sat down in a hard-backed chair. Mrs Randall remained standing, eyes downcast, mouth trembling slightly. She played with a lace handkerchief in her hands, wringing it as if it were wet.

"My husband..." Her voice trailed away and she sniffed loudly.

By now, Cole was possessed with such a sense of foreboding that he could barely speak. His voice creaked and croaked as he said, "Please. Tell me what has happened."

Her face came up and he could see she was crying, the tears rolling unchecked. "They've gone, Reuben."

He shook his head in dumb incomprehension.

"My husband is a captain in the regiment. He was approached by a sickly private who told him he wished to visit the doctor and receive some medicine for his ailment, but that he could not get an answer. My husband was at first a little put-out, wondering why this private could not gain entry to the surgery, go around the back, and rap on the windows. Eventually, Nigel – my husband – accompanied the private. Sure enough, the place appeared empty, so he took charge and ordered other men to force an entry." She suddenly broke down, pressing the handkerchief to her face as she collapsed into a padded chair opposite to where Cole sat. "They were in there. All three of them."

Cole held his breath, not daring to hear what it was this woman had to say next.

"They were dead, Reuben. The doctor, his wife and... sweet Jesus, the girl, Penny. All dead. I'm so sorry, Reuben. So very sorry."

She collapsed into tears then, unable to contain her emotions any longer, and Cole sat, numb with the enormity of what he'd heard, the news too dreadful to register in his confused mind. Dead? How could they be dead? All of them, the whole family? It simply was not possible! His voice broke as he managed the question, "How?"

Shaking her head, Mrs Randall stared at him in abject horror. "They'd... We *don't know*, Reuben. The colonel took it upon himself to go immediately to Camp Nelson where there is another doctor, a Major Steiner, something of an expert so I understand. On his return, a full examination will be made. Their quarters are sealed in case it is something catching. Until there has been a full investigation, all we can do is wait."

As if in a daze, Reuben returned to his quarters, giving up a small prayer of thanks that he had already completed his report. He was in no mood or desire to do anything but roll over and lie in his bunk. As various troops entered the bunkhouse after their duties were over, none disturbed him, all of them falling into awkward silence. Perhaps they already knew. News travelled fast through the camp.

He could not concentrate on anything, his mind a wrung-out rag of conflicting emotion. One thing worried him, however, more than anything else. It gnawed away at the very fibre of his being. Why had Danebridge not mentioned any of it to him? Why had he told Cole that the colonel had gone to Camp Nelson to review battle orders rather than the truth of him seeking out Doctor Steiner? Was it a genuine mistake, or had the colonel expressly forbade the lieutenant to refrain from discussing the events openly with Cole? Finding no answer, Cole, at long last, managed to push the thoughts to the back of his mind and drifted off to troubled sleep.

CHAPTER FOURTEEN

He woke before dawn and went outside. The camp was still, nobody yet stirring. The only sign of activity was a lone sentry standing on the ramparts looking out across the grey, cold fields. Cole gazed at him wistfully, wishing he was that sentry right now. Thoughts of Penny came once more into his mind... her face, the sound of her voice, her laughter. Those eyes, always dancing with the light of inner happiness. What had happened to extinguish it? Sickness? But, for all three to have been stricken, that would mean it was something contagious, and therefore, a danger for everyone in the camp. Surely, the colonel would have imposed some form of quarantine, or even abandonment of the camp?

Blowing out a loud blast of air, he rubbed his face with his hands and decided to take his horse and ride out to the only remaining place that could offer him any form of solace – the open range.

He rode for a long time. This was not a land he felt at home with. Too many trees, too much grass. He longed for the open sweep of the plains, the high mountains, the promise of returning to his family ranch. He would have liked to have taken Penny back home, introduce her to his father, and show everyone how proud he was.

Youth cannot give way to age and experience until time has passed. As he reined in his horse and stood staring out towards a cluster of trees, he could hear the faint sound of water, smell the sweetness in the air. And everywhere, in the grass, the sky, the way the shadows played amongst the undulating landscape, he saw her face. Those dancing eyes, that beautiful smile, and her voice, honey-drenched, sweet, soft and true. Penny.

In a rush, all of his false bravado, his self-control, strength evaporated before he could stop himself. He burst into tears and wept uncontrollably for all that he had lost. His old life, his mother, Penny. Everything combined to swallow him in an enveloping cloud of gloom and despair.

Would life ever be the same again?

His return to camp was slow and steady. Deep in thought, he needed to know the truth of what had happened. He needed the colonel to return.

As Danebridge had forecast, Cairn's trial was a formality. Cole sat in silence at the back, arms crossed, staring into the distance, vaguely aware of what went on around him. Nothing much had any great meaning for him anymore, but he did his best to listen. A young second-lieutenant defended Cairns with admirable zeal, but the evidence proved too overwhelming for the residing officers – two gruff-looking majors sporting huge handlebar mous-taches and bored expressions, together with a captain of artillery whose vicious, livid scar running across the ruin of his left cheek took everyone's attention – to ponder on their judgement for more than a few minutes.

Cairns duly stood as the sentence was announced. He gave

no reaction at the news of his impending doom the following morning. Without a glance, he turned on his heels, and his escort took him back to his cell.

Desperate to leave the oppressive atmosphere within the makeshift courtroom, Cole stepped outside into the afternoon sunshine and took a moment to breathe in the fresh air. He wandered away from the parade ground and the steady pounding of hammers and the screech of saws as a bunch of soldiers in shirt-sleeves worked on erecting a scaffold. Cole had little desire to contemplate or, indeed, witness Cairn's execution on the following morning. He'd had enough of death for now.

He called in at Danebridge's quarters only to be told the lieutenant had gone away. Perhaps he had ridden across to Camp Nelson to rendezvous with Colonel Astley. The sentry at the door did not know, and his expression told Cole he did not care.

"So, who is in command?"

"Lieutenant Danebridge was never in charge."

"All right, but the question still stands."

The sentry gave him a dark look. "Major Knowles."

"He was at the trial, I think."

"Trial?"

"Court martial, then. Cairns was sentenced. He's to hang tomorrow."

The sentry clicked his tongue. "They should feed him to the dogs. How many of our boys has he sent to an early grave, eh?"

"Too many. But, at least it ends soon enough."

"Until we go up against the Rebs again and get another ass-kicking."

"You think we will?"

"Things ain't been going well, have they? President promised all sorts when this fury broke out, but I have yet to see any good coming out of all this killin'. You fought in battle?"

"I'm a scout, so I ain't seen fighting in the field, but," he put in quickly as he noted the sentry's expression turning sour, "I have been in a number of firefights. I know all about killing."

The sentry gave him a long look from head to toe and back again. "You ain't much older than a newly laid chick. How come you been fighting?"

Cole shrugged. "I've had to learn fast. I ain't proud of anything I've done, but the killing has taught me a great deal."

"Has it, by God?" The man looked away, suddenly serious. "Well, I got to admit, I ain't seen anything as yet. Only marching and foraging. Ain't seen so much as a Reb pair of boots on a porch step."

"Disappointed, are you?"

"Good Lord Almighty, no! I will be a happy man if, when this sorry mess is over, I can say I never did fire my musket in anger. I'm scared and I don't mind telling you." He frowned deeply. "You scared?"

Cole realised that for all his bravado and gruffness, the sentry couldn't have been more than a couple of years older than himself. "All the time."

This confession seemed to give the sentry a great deal of relief, and he actually smiled for the first time since they started speaking to one another. "I am off duty in the hour. I'd like to invite you for a quiet drink later if you would do me the honour?"

Cole tipped his hat. He was full of sadness and grief for Penny, and wasn't sure if he could stomach an evening of relaxation. The thought made him feel guilty. "I have duties of my own, I'm sorry to say."

"Well, another time, then? My names is Barnes. Finias Barnes." He stuck out his hand. Cole took it, introduced himself and walked away to his barrack room feeling heavy and sad.

Horrible flashing images of screaming faces, grinning faces, ashen, death-white faces filled his dreaming moments and he awoke with a start, sitting bolt upright, awash with sweat. In the corner, Penny stood, clad in a white robe, her face obscured by a veil, hand reaching out to him, imploring him, "Reuben," she whispered, "Reuben, I miss you..."

Swinging away from this vision, his guts twisting inside him, his mother stood close to his bedside, her face so concerned, her eyes wide and filled with tears. "My son, my son..."

Throwing back his covers, Cole staggered backwards, lost in the darkness and the horrors he witnessed, as bells clanged louder than anything else, a constant, unending cacophony of sound accompanied by a single, anxious, startled voice, "To arms, men! Call out the guard!"

"Cole, what in the hell?"

He turned and cried out as a tall soldier gripped him by the shoulder, "What are you doing?"

Shaking himself more fully awake, Cole realised that his waking nightmare was at least partially a reality. Men were running around the barracks room, pulling on boots and tunics and scrambling for muskets as panic descended.

Watching it all as if from a distance, Cole jumped as the main door burst open, a figure filling the space, roaring, "Get yourselves assembled on the parade ground immediately!"

Less than five minutes later, the centre of the camp was filled with the hastily assembled men of the regiment, sergeants checking the lines, several men quickly buttoning up tunics, adjusting trousers, an expectant murmur rippling through them.

"Atten –*shun*!" roared a massive sergeant-major flanking a group of officers waiting patiently for the men to settle. Instantly, the voices stopped and the soldiers drew themselves up straight. Cole, standing a little way off, noted that the sergeant-major was his trainer, Arnoldson. He also noted that the officer stepping forward was Major Knowles.

"Listen carefully, men," the major began, his eyes scanning the assembled soldiers. "The prisoner, Cairns, has broken free and is even now making his way back to the enemy lines." The murmuring started up again. Arnoldson glared and everyone stopped. "This means the Rebs, once Cairns has told them of our situation, will be on their way here in double-quick time. We are, therefore, to ready ourselves to a high state of preparedness. Scouts will be sent out, artillery readied, muskets cleaned and primed. We are but one small part of the Army of the Potomac, but we are unarguably the most vulnerable. There are but eight-hundred of us here, and a successful full-scale assault will expose the army's flank and push it back into the sea. The entire success of General McClellan's plan to rout the rebel forces could well rest on how we respond to this situation. I know we will prevail, men. God is with us, and I am assured of your abilities to win through!"

As one, the men roared out their approval and lifted their voices in wild cheers, many brandishing their muskets, some throwing their kepis high into the air.

Knowles watched this patiently, nodding with satisfaction at the battalion's reactions. In a quieter voice, he said, "Sergeants, take charge of your companies and carry out your orders."

He swung away and, accompanied by two other officers, crossed over to where Cole stood.

"Well, Cole, are you ready?"

Without knowing what the major was referring to, Cole puffed out his chest. "Ready and willing, sir."

"Good man. You're the only scout we have and yours is a heavy burden, but you must track Cairns down before he reaches the enemy lines."

"And, bring him back, sir?"

Knowles looked away. One of the other officers stepped up. "Whatever it takes, Cole. Our only concern is that he is prevented from informing the Rebs of our situation."

"I understand, sir."

"You've proved yourself more than once, Cole," said Knowles. "I know you will succeed. You leave as soon as you are ready."

Cole saluted and waited for the officers to move away before he allowed himself to relax. He was a little surprised to see Arnoldson standing there, staring.

"Do we know how he managed to escape?"

Arnoldson took a step closer. "It seems he had insider help." A shake of his head. "No doubt the accomplice who has been furnishing him with our plans all along. Danebridge."

Cole drew in a breath and gave himself a few moments to recover from the shock of this revelation. "They'll be desperate and dangerous now that their deceptions have been exposed. I'll need help if I'm to bring them both in."

Arnoldson poked out the tip of his tongue and ran it across his top lip. "I've been ordered to supply you with an effective rifle with the capability to hit a target at over six hundred yards if fired by a trained sharpshooter."

He paused. Cole held his stare. "I ain't no assassin if that's what you're implying, Sergeant."

"No, but they have to be stopped, Cole. If not, we could be at the brunt of a devastating attack."

"So, that's the help I've got, is it? A rifle?"

"A damned good one, Cole. Maybe not as good as the one the Rebs are being supplied with, or even some of our other troops, but it has been adapted and it's the best we have at the moment. You meet me at the firing range as soon as you are able, and you can fire off a few rounds and get used to it, so to speak." He arched a single eyebrow. "Talking of practise, I'm guessing you've kept up the little tricks I taught you?"

"Every day."

"Good. We can test you out on that, too."

The sergeant turned on his heels and marched off, leaving Cole to reconsider what exactly his role in this army was.

CHAPTER FIFTEEN

For the fifth time, the crack of the rifle rang out across the firing range, the bullet slapping unerringly into the centre of the target. Cole was prone, a model 1843 Luttich Carbine in his grip. Arnoldson told him it was owned by Major Knowles, who had personally entrusted it into Cole's capable hands. Such a decision seemed well-proven. The first shot had wandered to the left, meaning Cole had to readjust the sights. Now, with everything set up successfully, the subsequent shots were perfect. He'd increased the range every time, and now, with the target placed at eight hundred paces, the bullet hit the target directly in the centre.

"Dead-eye," muttered Arnoldson, who was viewing each shot through a set of German-made binoculars. As Cole got up from his position, Arnoldson handed him the eyeglasses and their case. "Take these. A gift, if you like."

Cole stared down at the wonderfully engineered piece of equipment. "So, I'll ask this again. I'm alone in this endeavour?"

"We cannot spare a single man, Cole. If you fail..." He shrugged.

Releasing a long sigh, Cole returned the binoculars to their case and snapped it shut. "I'll set out right away. Do we know when Cairns broke out?"

"No. His flight was not discovered until the guard on duty was due to be relieved. That would be at around four this morning when the alarm was raised.

"The guard was overpowered?"

Arnoldson turned down the corners of his mouth. "The guard was dead, his throat slit. Probably by Danebridge."

The silence spread out between them.

"Who was it?" Cole asked at last.

"A young soldier called Barnes." He stopped and frowned.

Rubbing his forehead. Cole struggled to prevent himself from collapsing as the blood drained from him. Another death. He felt as if invisible hands were squeezing his throat, strangling him.

"Cole? Did you know him?"

In despair, Cole dragged his hand over his face in a vain attempt to wipe away the horrors threatening to crush him. "Finias? I knew him... only slightly. But, we spoke together. He'd invited me to take a drink with him and I... Dear God, to murder him like that."

"They have no scruples, that is for sure."

Gathering up his rifle, Cole made as if to turn away, but was brought up sharply by Arnoldson's gruff voice. "I still need to see if you can handle Cairns without resort to firearms."

"Not now, Sergeant. This quest has now become somewhat more urgent."

"Even so." Arnoldson bunched his fist. "Take a swing."

Blowing out his breath, Cole put down the rifle and the binoculars, threw away his hat and went into a half-crouch. "Damn you."

"That's right, damn me. Now, take a swing."

It was brief, but anyone observing would have been impressed. Cole feinted with a long jab, checked himself and, as Arnoldson prepared to counter, Cole danced to the side, cracked his boot into the big man's knee and felled him as he buckled forward with a swinging left.

Picking up his belongings, Cole gave the sergeant a withering glance. "If you were Cairns, I'd break your neck. But, you ain't, so I'll just leave you to eat the dirt. So long, Sergeant."

Groaning, Arnoldson rolled over onto his back and blinked towards the sky. "Jeez..."

Cole didn't bother to answer, and strode away to the camp livery stables to ready his horse.

There was mad, unchecked mayhem back at camp. At least two dozen men were preparing several six-pounder artillery pieces whilst around them, soldiers mingled, rushing here and there, many scaling ladders to man the ramparts of the encircling fort. Already, spotters were positioned in the watchtower, telescopes scanning the distant horizon. What took Cole's attention, however, was the sight of Major Knowles in deep conversation with two other officers and, slightly behind them, Mrs Randall. He caught her eye and she rushed over, dabbing her eyes with a handkerchief.

"Reuben," she gasped, seeming to block his approach. "Reuben. It is Major Steiner's orderly, a Lieutenant Pace. My husband has returned with him and they..."

She broke down and Cole, momentarily forgetting any propriety, took her by the shoulders. "Mrs Randall? What is it?"

"The doctor, Lieutenant Pace, I mean, he has examined the remains... Reuben, I'm sorry," she sniffed loudly and stared into his eyes with such concern that Cole once more experienced that awful feeling of imminent collapse engulfing him. "Penny and her family, they... Oh, dear Lord, there is no other to tell you this. They were murdered, Reuben. All three of them. *Murdered.*"

Cole dropped his hands and rammed a fist into his mouth to prevent himself from screaming out his despair.

He wandered away as if he had entered another world, populated by himself alone. The real world continued around him, but he was no longer aware of it. He stumbled away towards the steps of the makeshift prison and collapsed upon them.

"Cole?"

The sound of his name forced him to look up. There stood Major Knowles, serious, concerned, eyebrows bristling, his look dark and unblinking. "Cole. I know you were friendly with..." He turned away, sighed. "We've spoken, and what we have come up with is a fairly horrific conclusion. The good doctor must have somehow discovered Danebridge's true identity. We know the Lieutenant visited the doctor's quarters, and it is clear what happened."

"Danebridge. He did it, he killed the entire..." Cole pressed his face into his hands.

"We now have an even more pressing situation, Cole. Not only is it imperative that Danebridge and Cairns are stopped, but we have fears for Colonel Astley. He must even now be travelling back from Camp Nelson with Doctor Steiner. If they were to encounter Danebridge and Cairns... Well, I do not need to explain to you what the outcome would be."

"No," said Cole, gathering himself, the twisting knot in his guts turning into a solid coil of steel. He stood up, set his teeth and growled, "I'll leave now, Major. And, I won't let you, or anyone else down."

He marched off towards the livery, eyes set straight ahead. Penny, dear Penny, their friendship so brief, so full of promise, was dead. Murdered. Assassin he may not be, but now he had every reason to put an end to this nightmare once and for all.

Revenge.

CHAPTER SIXTEEN

They were careless in their escape. Cole had little trouble picking up their trail. He forced himself to slow his pursuit, not wishing his desire for vengeance to cloud his judgment. On constant alert, he found the sweeping flow of the verdant land easy to navigate. The many trees afforded plenty of shade from the sun, and he grew to enjoy the ride, despite the reason for him being there.

In a tiny depression, he came across evidence of a camp. The remains of a rabbit lay amongst the blackened embers of the fire, and he recalled how the family of Shawnee had given him food not so very long ago. A stab of regret for not taking some provisions to them gave him pause to consider how, regardless of how pleasant this country was in comparison to his own homeland, life remained a struggle.

He moved on, making camp himself some hours later. He did not light a fire, but the air was mild, and a supper of hard-tack and water proved sufficient to ease the rumblings from deep within his guts.

The morning dawned cool and bright. He adjusted a burlap nosebag around his horse's neck. Filled with oats and barley, the mare probably ate better than he had. She was well-used to the bag and lowered it to the ground to munch through the contents with little difficulty. Cole wandered over to some nearby trees to relieve himself before stretching out his back.

He heard the unmistakeable sound of an approaching horse almost immediately. Hastily, he drew his Colt Dragoon – his second gun remained in one of the saddlebags back in his makeshift camp – and slowly lowered himself to one knee.

The approaching sound confused him. He knew for certain that Cairns and Danebridge could not have doubled back. There was little chance that they were aware of his pursuit, so this had to be someone else. No Shawnee or any other Native would be so careless in their approach. Anyone else out here at this time must therefore be...

He almost cried out when the rider came into view. Bent over on his saddle, one hand hanging limply by his side, a dried blood trail clearly visible, with the other gripping the reins, the man was in some distress. Bareheaded and head down, nevertheless, he was easily recognisable as Colonel Astley.

Holstering his gun, Cole burst through the surrounding trees and ran towards his commanding officer. The horse took fright and almost bolted. The Colonel, alerted by his mount's sudden frenzy, brought it under control with consummate skill and turned his face towards Cole, who stood two paces from him, breathing hard, but grinning broadly.

"Dear Lord," croaked the Colonel, "I thought my end had come!"

Edging forward, Cole took in more of the Colonel's condition and saw, much to his alarm, that the man's skin was a deathly pallor, drained of blood. His eyes were red-rimmed, lips blue. As Colonel Astley forced a smile, it became apparent he was suffering as his otherwise friendly expression transformed into a grimace of pure agony.

"I've been shot more than once, Cole, and I'm close to death, but by God, it is good to see you!"

With that, all the strength which had borne him this far left him and, barely conscious, he slumped sideways. Cole caught him and gently eased him to the ground. Taking a brief moment to secure the horse to a nearby tree branch before returning to the Colonel, Cole knelt beside him, supporting the man's head. He spoke with as much reassurance as he could. "I'll tend to you, Colonel. I have water in my camp, and I'll rustle up some strong coffee. I have learned how to make and apply a poultice to your wound. I'll see you through."

The Colonel's eyes barely managed to flicker. "God bless you, Cole, but I'm afeared my strength may not see me through to the end of the morning."

"Nonsense, Colonel! All I need you to do is hold on. You hear me?" The slightest of nods came, which sufficed for a reply, and gave Cole some encouragement. "Hold on."

The return journey to the army camp was slow. Every piece of uneven ground, every hidden rock or tree root which forced the horse to shy away, slip or stumble caused the colonel to moan. Teeth set on edge, all Cole could do was put his face forward and pray for the miles to disappear.

Eventually, the camp entrance came into view. The sentries, catching sight of Cole and his burden, rushed forward and helped their commanding officer to shelter.

Soon, as Cole saw to the horses, Major Knowles caught up with him, face serious and concerned. One look at Cole's grim expression caused him to fall into a deeper pit of despair.

"He's going to die, isn't he?"

Cole could not bring himself to meet the Major's eyes. Instead, he stared to the ground as he kicked at an imaginary stone. "I think so, Major."

"Damn it, and damn them!" He punched his palm with his other fist. "I'm assuming it was them – Cairns and Danebridge – who did this?"

"Can't see it being anyone else."

"And, what of them? Did you come across them?"

Cole shook his head. "There were signs, but then the Colonel came into view. So, I'm thinking..." He blew out a loud breath. "I'm guessing they must have bushwhacked him as he travelled back from Nelson. As soon as I've rested my horse, I'll go back out and find 'em. They ride with the contemptuous arrogance of ones who believe they are invulnerable. I'll catch them, bring 'em in."

"I'm giving you two men, Cole. I can ill-afford it. News came in while you were away. It's looking bleak. The Rebs' new commander has given them a renewed sense of belief. Our troops are being pressed hard, and many units are in retreat. Time is not on our side, Cole."

He moved away, and Cole, continuing to stare at the ground, knew that the reckoning was close.

CHAPTER SEVENTEEN

C ole delayed his departure for one extra day. The previous
evening, Colonel Astley gave up his struggle, and Cole,
along with the entire regiment, stood in silence to pay their
respects as the Commander was buried with all ceremonial
honours.

Later, with the overriding mood of the camp grim, Cole met
the two soldiers ordered to accompany him on his quest to bring
Cairns to justice. They were young, unseasoned privates, perhaps
one or two years older than his purported eighteen years. By the
look of their smooth faces, Cole wondered if they, too, had lied
to get themselves into uniform.

Their conversation was brief and, with their horses well
prepared with rations, water, ammunition, the ubiquitous blanket
roll, and extra food stored in Cole's saddlebags for his Indian
friends, the three men set out in the late afternoon. No one bade
them farewell or wished them luck... not even Major Knowles,
who had remained in his quarters since the Colonel's burial. The
rumour which went round said he was a heavy drinker, so no
doubt he was finding solace in the bottom of a whisky glass.

As before, Cole picked up the trail and, after reaching the

spot where he had come across Colonel Astley, they made camp. They ate a hearty supper, Cole relieved not to be consuming the usual helping of hard-tack and biscuits. One of the men, who had introduced himself as Campbell, fried up slices of cured bacon, which they all munched down with relish. Anderton, the second soldier, took first watch, and the night passed without incident.

Setting out early the following morning, they crossed rolling fields, steering clear of homesteads and the occasional farm. Soon, Cole recognised the area as the one where the group of Shawnee lived. He pulled up his horse on the rise and stared down into the depression where the Shawnee had greeted him, fed him, and showed him a kindness he believed he would never experience again.

"What is that?" asked Anderton drawing up alongside.

Cole's eyes narrowed as he stared at the view.

"Whatever it was," said Campbell, stroking his mount's neck, "it ain't no more."

A stab of pain hit Cole in the throat. Squeezing his eyes to prevent a tear from tumbling down his cheek, Cole flicked the reins and cautiously moved forward.

The rank smell of burning wood hung heavy in the air as Cole eased his horse through the remnants of the shattered Shawnee camp. He dismounted and, drawing his revolver, went into one of the huts, the only one whose roof was still intact. The rest were gutted skeletons of what they had once been, oil black streaks staining the outer walls.

The tang of death was everywhere.

Pausing for a moment outside the entrance to the intact hut, Cole pulled in a breath and ducked inside.

The children were there. Three of them, their tiny bodies splayed out across the ground, their faces frozen in the ghastly, waxen visage of the dead. Beside them, their mothers, bloodied, with clothes dishevelled. A single warrior sat propped up in the far corner, his eyes wide, the huge hole in his throat bearing testimony to what had happened.

"Hey, Cole," cried one of the others, "there are bodies out here."

Swallowing down the sobs threatening to rip out of his mouth, Cole went outside and went to where the others stood, mesmerised, staring at a group of warriors shot to pieces, their bodies splattered with blood.

"You know these people?"

Cole looked up and forced himself to meet Campbell's questioning gaze. "When they were alive, yes."

Taking note of the dangerous tone in Cole's voice, the others did not pursue their questioning.

It took some time, and Cole, not long in this land and its ways, did not know how best to proceed, but he decided to bury the children in shallow graves beside their mothers. He did not know who was who, of course, but he was assured that whatever did happen after death, they would somehow seek each other out. The warriors were buried a little distance away.

His two companions helped, and did so in silence. When they had finished, they all sat down in a small glade overhung with trees, drank water from their canteens, and stared into the distance.

"Seems to me," said Campbell at long last, "that people is people, no matter what their colour might be." He turned his gaze towards Cole. "In the end, we all return to the earth."

"What we did here, burying 'em," added Anderton, "it was the right thing."

The stillness between them continued as they set out once more. Cole picked up the trail fairly soon, dropping from his saddle to investigate the signs in the ground. It was proving more difficult than previously due to the amount of time that had passed since the two men set out on their escape. It was clear to Cole, however, that their detour to ransack the small Shawnee homestead had delayed them sufficiently for the signs to remain. He stood up, face set to the west. He sighed deeply. "They're going to make the Reb camp before we overtake them."

"Then, we've lost 'em," said Anderton. "We can't go into the camp, Cole." He tugged at the buttons of his army blouse. "They'll catch sight of us within two hundred yards and kill us."

"Yeah, but I ain't wearing no blue," said Cole without turning to the others.

"What is it you're proposing, Cole?" asked Campbell, his voice sounding strained.

Cole turned around. "I ain't asking anything of you, neither of you. You were ordered to accompany me, but even if you did take off your uniforms, the Rebs will suss you out in about a minute and all that we've done so far will be for nothin'. So, we'll carry on for a while longer, make camp and then I'll continue to where the Rebs are camped. You can wait for me to return."

"And, if you don't?"

Cole smiled ruefully towards Anderton. "Then, you go back and tell the Major I'm dead."

The two young soldiers exchanged worried looks.

"For all I know," said Cole without reacting to their obvious discomfort, "the Rebs have more than likely moved on. From what the Major told me, the Reb forces are on the move. They have a new general and are full of renewed energy."

"Then, there is no point in anything, is there?" Anderton kicked at the ground. "I volunteered to fight, keep the Union together. I believed our cause was a righteous one, but all that I've experienced so far, I ain't so sure."

Cole shrugged. "There's more than a point to it for me. I couldn't give a damn about Jed Stuart's plans, or who is fighting who. The whole stinking thing is a sorry mess if you ask me. But, what Danebridge did back in our camp, and what he and Cairns did to those Shawnees... No, this has gone beyond army orders, boys. I'm gonna kill 'em, kill 'em both."

Sometime later, they stopped and lay down on a slight rise. Peering through his eyeglasses, Cole viewed long lines of

Confederate troops marching across the land. Even with the lens, the figures were not much more than tiny specs of dust, but he knew what it meant. Rolling over, he said to the others, "They're on the move. Can't see much cavalry, so I'm guessing Stuart is already making for the outflanking move we predicted."

"So, what'll we do about Cairns?"

Cole returned the eyeglasses to their case. "I'll have to circle the column, do my best to infiltrate it."

"That's suicide, Cole, and you know it," said Anderton.

"I ain't got much choice. I want you two to make camp here. I'll get back as soon as I can."

"You can't," said Campbell, something akin to panic coming into his voice. "For God's sake, Cole, you're taking too much of a risk and that's—"

"I'm touched by your concern, fellas, I truly am, but this is something I have to do, and do it alone. At least *try* to do." He moved across to his horse, attached the eyeglasses to his saddle and mounted up. "Give me two days. If I'm not back by then, return to the camp and let the Major know what's happening. It's the only option left to us. The Rebs are still miles away, and are moving fairly slowly, so even two days should see everyone safe with time enough to prepare."

There was no answer from either man, both staring at the young scout with looks of despair engrained into their faces. He gave them a wry smile and kicked his horse into a steady walk.

He did not look back.

CHAPTER EIGHTEEN

Despite knowing the Confederate forces were far away, Cole rode steadily and with great care, scanning the surrounding ground, looking for any sign of the two men he hunted. It was as he did so that he came across the unmistakeable signs of violence. Patches of blood interlaced the broken ground, grass and crushed branches. In a shallow dip, he came across the body of a uniformed soldier. On closer inspection, Cole noted the insignia, dismounted and inspected the body. He'd obviously been dead for some time, the skin blackened, the flies already making a feast of the area where the gunshots had ripped into him. Delving inside the dead man's tunic, he found neatly folded documents, and he read them, his heart sinking with every word.

It was Major Steiner, the doctor whom Colonel Astley had gone to fetch from Fort Nelson. Cole rocked back on his heels. So, this was where the firefight took place. Where Astley had been mortally wounded.

He pushed the document into his pocket and stood up. He scanned the surroundings. Something was disquieting about the place. Trees and undergrowth formed the perfect boundary to where the body lay amongst the tall grass, but could do little to penetrate the pervading atmosphere of death. There was something...

Drawing his revolver, he moved through the grass. In parts, it came up to his knees. This would be a good place to lie in wait, preparing to ambush an unwary passer-by, he mused. Stopping, he listened. There was nothing, strangely, not even the reassuring sound of birdsong. They, too, it would seem, preferred to keep away from this place.

He found it not two minutes later.

Danebridge, his broken body lying in a horrible attitude, one claw-like hand raised, frozen in a final gesture, perhaps pleading for his life. Cole, standing there, taking in the grim sight, felt nothing save for regret, regret that it was not he who had ended Danebridge's life. Astley had done this for him, but at least had sent one of the traitors to meet a final reckoning with his maker!

All Cole needed to do now was find Cairns.

He heard the approaching horses before he spotted them. They were moving at a tremendous pace, charging down on an individual a short distance ahead of them. With little time to react, Cole turned his horse and urged it towards a cluster of rocks and bushes. Behind, the crack of pistol shots sounded too close for comfort, and Cole was already dropping to the ground before his mount came to a full stop. Acting quickly, he pulled out the Luttich carbine from its sheath attached to the saddle, fell to one knee and sighted down the barrel.

He gasped when he saw who the pursued man was.

Lester.

Rolling his shoulders, Cole settled into his aim. The group of riders in pursuit, some grey-clad, were clearly Confederate troopers. Without another thought, Cole blew one of them clean out of the saddle. The others reacted instantly, reining in their horses, shocked and surprised by the blast. Whirling around in a frenzy of screaming horses and kicked-up ground, they dismounted, firing off shots wildly in no particular direction.

Cole shot a second man and paused, lowering his weapon, watching Lester drawing closer. He reined in his horse, terrified eyes glaring at Cole. "Where the hell did you—"

"Get to cover," said Cole, drawing his Dragoon. He stood and fired off round after round towards the hastily dismounting enemy troopers. He backed off and dropped down behind a large rock as Lester ushered his horse into the cover of the trees. Breathing hard, the captain knelt next to Cole.

"I never thought I'd live to see you again, Cole."

Carefully reloading the Luttich before turning to the Dragoon, Cole concentrated on the job in hand for the moment. As he tapped in powder, ball and percussion cap, Cole eventually settled his eyes on the captain. Blood seeped out from under the cuff of Lester's jacket, and there was dried blood on the man's mouth and nose, his eyes blackened, his forehead bright red. "Looks like you've taken something of a beating, Cap'n."

Lester chuckled humourlessly. "You could say that."

"Who did it? Cairns?"

"How you know that?"

"Call it a wild guess."

A bullet pinged off the top of the rock, forcing both men to duck down despite the bullet ricocheting out of harm's way.

Drawing his pistol, Lester checked his load, put the barrel over the rock's rim and fired off three quick shots. Several responding slugs slapped into the rock, sending up jagged flakes of stone. "They've got us pinned down here, Cole. We'll have to make a run for the horses and ride out of here."

"They'll flank us," said Cole, with his back to the boulder, "and cut us off. We'll never make it to the horses."

"So, what do we do?"

"How many are they?"

"Eight or nine. You hit two, so... Listen, why don't I draw

them off by going in amongst the trees? I'll skirt around the sides and flank *them*."

"Same problem. Even if I cover you, they'll already be in position to cut you off." He strained to his left to try and gain a view of the enemy troopers. He spotted several, crouching and moving from cover to cover, brought up the Luttich and winged one in the shoulder just before he dived out of view.

"That's a fine-looking weapon you have there," said Lester.

"It's Russian and has a much greater range than anything else available back at the camp."

"But, what do you need it for?"

"Don't ask." Cole chanced another glance. The enemy troopers were scampering ever closer.

"Cole," said Lester in a tense, nervous sounding voice, "I have three more shots left. I have no more powder, so we have little choice. I'll lead them off. Trust me."

"No, that wouldn't work. I need to break cover, Cap'n. I'll give you the Luttich. Cover me and I'll—"

"Damn it, Cole, I said I'd do that!"

Shaking his head, Cole screwed up his mouth. "You're wounded, Cap'n, as well as suffering from the beating. You're putting on a brave show of none of it mattering much, but I can see how much pain you're in. You'll never make it."

For a reply, Lester ran a hand over his sallow-coloured face. "Cairns got wind of me almost as soon as he rode into the Reb camp. Up until then, I'd fooled 'em, mingled, listened. I was wrong to think I could outwit Cairns, however. He spotted me and shadowed me without my knowing. They grabbed me as I relaxed in the mess hall. They took me to their commander after beating the living hell out of me to try and get any information. They threw me in one of the stables, thinking I was incapable of doing much, but I managed to break free..." He shook his head. "Cairns shot me in the arm as I made a run for it from the camp. Then, all the furies from hell were on my tail. I had no idea you were here, and now I've dropped you right in it. I'm sorry, Cole. I truly am."

"Is Cairns with 'em?"

A dark cast fell over Lester's features. "Yes, indeed, the murdering... Damn it, Cole, I have it – Jeb Stuart's plans. And now, everything I have managed to find out will be lost because of my own stupidity."

"Cap'n, we ain't done for yet."

"Maybe not, but if I don't get the plans to the Colonel, all of it would have been for nothing."

"The Colonel is dead, Cap'n. I'm pretty sure that was down to Cairns, too."

Lester seemed to collapse within himself and he slumped against the rock. "That's it, then. We're done for."

"I have two troopers waiting for me back at our makeshift camp. If the worse happens and we don't make it, they'll get word to our men. It won't all have been for nothing."

"And, those men will march straight into Stuart's ambush."

Cole blew out a breath. The time had come for action, not words. "Cap'n, you just hold on here and cover me with the Luttich." He drew his Paterson and hefted it and the Dragoon in his hands. "I'll see you shortly."

He readied himself, took a quick look over the boulder, cursed and grunted. "They're moving in. It's now or never."

"Damn..." Lester took the Luttich and flicked up the rear sight. He winced. "My hand... Cole, God help us."

"Yeah." He winked, jumped to his feet and ran.

CHAPTER NINETEEN

He saw them, perhaps three or four enemy troopers, advancing towards him, but he could not afford to stand and shoot. Bent double, he weaved left and right, making himself as small a target as possible. He dare not stop. Behind him, Lester worked the Luttich as best he could, but nowhere near as fast as Cole would have wished. It was clear that the Captain, due to his wounded hand, was struggling, but there was no other choice to make. If they remained behind the rock, those flanking them would have had an easy time of shooting them dead. So, Cole ran, and as he did so, he became aware that the Luttich was no longer giving him cover.

When the bullets started flying around him, he dived for cover, thinking that Lester must have either run out of bullets or had been shot himself. Either way, Cole knew that the end was close. Scrambling through the undergrowth, his only thought now was to give himself a chance, no matter how slight, to confront Cairns and somehow bring closure to this whole sorry episode.

A bullet smacked into the ground inches from his head. He rolled over, and another bullet scorched his hair... it was so close.

"Give it up, Cole," came the voice he knew so well.

Desperate now, he went to bring up his Paterson, but already, Cairns was beside him, his bulk blocking out the sky. He was laughing as he kicked away Cole's hand, sending his gun flying away.

Pressing his own pistol hard against Cole's forehead, Cairns hissed, "Time to end your sorry existence, boy. Put the other gun down."

There was little point in resisting, so Cole let the Dragoon drop to the ground. A strong hand hauled him to his feet, the knee erupting into his groin before he had a chance to defend himself. He crumpled, the searing pain accompanying the overwhelming wave of nausea, which conquered his senses and his strength. He rolled around groaning, hands clasped between his legs, the red-hot tears momentarily blinding him.

"I've been looking forward to this," said Cairn's voice, distant, but distinct enough for Cole to recognise the man's joyful victory.

Brought to his feet again, Cole hung in the man's grip. He gazed into those malevolent eyes and cursed himself for not finding the strength to resist.

"Now, you're going to find out what it's like to suffer, Cole. You're a puny boy, and you ain't never gonna be strong enough to do anything about any of this."

He saw the fist being cocked, the grinning, taunting face, the gleeful look of triumph. He closed his eyes and the punch smashed into his cheek, the force of it throwing him backwards, his legs no longer able to work, his mind a jumbled mess of confusion, shame and frustration. He hit the earth hard, the air expelling loudly from his lungs.

It was over. He knew that. Despite the pain and the red mist blinding him, he was aware enough to know there was nothing he could do now. Cairns had won and the awful realisation of this undeniable truth brought him more pain than any blow. With gut-wrenching sobs engulfing him, he was suddenly a frightened, vulnerable teenager again, all of his fortitude and determination snuffed out.

"What's it feel like?" came that voice, the mocking tone, the easy confidence.

Despite everything, he sucked in several breaths and forced himself to his hands and knees. Almost instantly, a boot smashed into his side, hurling him over again into the dirt.

"Get up, boy, I ain't finished with you yet."

He caught sight of the Paterson, mere inches away. If only he could reach it, so tantalizingly close. He stretched out his fingers only for Cairns to step in and kick the gun deeper into the grass.

"You're annoying me now, boy," spat Cairns. He kicked away the Dragoon, sending it also well out of reach. He took hold of Cole again and lifted him to his feet.

"We ain't got time for any of this, Cairns," said somebody a little way off.

"You ride back," said Cairns, holding Cole so close, "I'm gonna enjoy myself."

"The other one's dead," a second voice said. "Kill this one and we'll go."

"No. Not yet."

Cole blinked through his tears. Hanging in Cairn's grip, he did his best to focus and managed to see nothing but the maniacal grin. If only he could be granted a few moments, a respite, so he could recover, then he'd make *him* suffer. He'd fight, the way he'd been taught, and he'd prove to everyone that he was no longer a boy.

But how, when Cairns held every advantage.

"Well, do it quickly, Cairns," said the first voice. "We're needed back at camp."

"Ah, hell," said Cairns, and drew back his fist in preparation for another punch.

Cole wasn't quite sure what happened next, but whatever it was, it gave him that wished-for respite.

Someone screamed. Another shouted. Guns barked, men died and Cairns, releasing Cole, turned away.

Falling to the ground, Cole sat on his backside, staring dumbly at his legs. A moment, that was all he needed. A moment to draw the oxygen deep into his lungs, to get his strength back, and to give Cairns a real contest.

"Get to cover," one of them shouted.

Looking up, bewildered but slowly grasping the details of what was occurring, Cole saw an arrow pierce a man's throat, watched him fall gagging, blood spurting. Another, fanning his revolver, went the same way, two arrows thudding into his chest. And then, like phantoms, they appeared, moving all around them. Hatchets and knives flashed.

They were under attack.

It did not take long and it was bloody and vicious, the Indians over-powering the terrified and confused Confederate troopers and dispatching them with gusto. By the time it was over, semi-naked, blood-spattered warriors stood as if mesmerised, huge eyes staring into the distance, consumed by their frenzied killing.

Their leader stepped forward. Cairns, who up until then remained unscathed, fell to his knees and took up moaning like a stricken animal. Hands clasped in front of him, he pleaded for his life.

Cole, managing to stand at last, gingerly pressed a shaking hand over his bruised face and forced a smile. "You cannot believe how good it is to see you," he said.

Cairns, emerging from his terror, snapped his head towards the young scout. "You know these savages?"

Cole ignored him and embraced the Shawnee leader.

Pushing himself away, the chief warrior became serious. "They came to our camp," he began, unable to keep the trembling from his voice. "They came when we were gone, roaming wide to hunt game, and they butchered our women and our children."

"I know." Cole hung his head, unable to meet the chief's gaze. "I buried them. I hope I have given them the honour they deserve."

"You are a good man," said the Shawnee, his eyes wet with tears. He turned his gaze upon Cairns. "His death will be slow and painful."

"Ah, God, *no!*" cried Cairns, climbing to his feet. "Cole, for pity's sake, if you know them, tell them – I'm to be taken back to your camp and tried."

"Looks like you've already been tried, Cairns. And, found guilty."

"You miserable cur," spat Cairns. "You're a coward and a weakling. I'd kill you now if I could – with my bare hands. Look at you, beaten, weeping like a baby girl. You're pathetic."

Dragging in a huge breath, Cole studied his hands, slowly turning them over. The shaking grew less. "I think you might have busted a rib of mine, Cairns. Bruised it badly, at least. And, my jaw..." He rubbed his chin and suddenly gave a laugh. "But, by God, I'll not be shamed by a murderer of women and children." He looked to the Shawnee. "This won't take long."

The other warriors, muttering amongst themselves, drew around in a small circle as Cole pulled off his shirt. He studied the vivid red and purple patch developing across his right side. "All right, Cairns, let's get to it."

"What? So, after I've beaten you to a pulp, your friends here will string me up?" He scoffed, hawked and spat. "No thanks."

"They won't do that." Cole sought affirmation from the Shawnee chief, who nodded once. "You beat me, you can return to your camp."

"I don't believe you. Beating you will be the easiest thing I've ever done."

"Let's see, shall we." Cole strode a few paces away to his left, bringing up his hands, palms out. "This time, I'll be ready for you, you treacherous dog."

Laughing out loud, Cairns went into a crouch. His limp was barely noticeable and caused him no loss of manoeuvrability as he bunched his fists and charged.

Cole waited. Prior to his training, he may have panicked, reacting too soon, swinging wild, wide punches which did more to exhaust himself than deliver damage to any opponent. Now, as Cairns closed in close, Cole dodged and moved, left fist hitting Cairns in the back of the neck, knee swinging up, throwing the man's head back. A right to the guts doubled Cairns up, and a short, sharp left smashed across his jaw. As he began to fall, Cole's right swung upwards again. He moved, he danced, he threw jabs and hooks, sometimes to the body, sometimes to the face. Cairns, blood-spattered, breathing hard and yelling with frustration was strong. He did not go down. Any of Cole's blows would have dropped a lesser opponent. Not so Cairns. He gathered himself and attacked again. His blows swung, but hit only air, and as Cole continued to throw out his fists, the accumulation of so many punches took their toll.

But, Cole, too, was finding it hard. Each thrown punch took too much out of him. The beating he'd taken previously, and the sheer physical exertion and determination of dodging and swerving, drained him of his strength. He was tiring, and Cairns, sensing the change, readied himself.

All at once, the tide had turned. Cairns charged in low, head down, and slammed into Cole's midriff with the power of an enraged bull. A blast of air rushed out of the young scout's mouth and he buckled. A long, lazy left smashed into his jaw and dumped him to the ground.

He lay, gulping in replacement air, desperate to gather himself.

Cairns weakened beyond anything he'd ever experienced, could do nothing but stand and watch. Blood trickled from the lattice-work of wounds across his face. He gently pushed an index finger into his mouth, exploring his teeth. "You've broken some, Cole," he said through lips so swollen his words sounded distorted, "and now, I'm gonna break you."

He took a step and cried out. The old wound, where Cole had shot him all that time ago, took that moment to rear up again, and he staggered, bending to clutch at where the bullet had penetrated. Falling, breath wheezing, his bloated, bloodied face screwed up in agony.

Cole took his chance.

Despite his own weakened state, he got to his feet, clenching and unclenching fists red-raw from landing so many blows against Cairn's hard jaw, and launched a powerful kick which struck Cairns under the chin, hurling him backwards.

Pouncing, Cole threw in several more punches until Cairn's face resembled something akin to a ruptured, over-ripe pumpkin.

About to slam in a final devastating blow, the Shawnee chief grabbed his arm and held him back. "Enough, my friend," he said. "You have proven yourself in this fight."

Cole, knowing the sense of it, relaxed and stepped away. He watched as the Indians bundled Cairns over the back of a horse and readied themselves to move on.

"We have nowhere to go but to the reservation," said the chief, his face etched with despair. "I doubt we shall meet again."

"I'll always remember your kindness."

"And I, too, will keep your friendship forever in my heart."

They moved away in silence, the only sound the pathetic mumbling of Cairns begging them to let him go, for Cole to help him, how sorry he was, how he knew now that the young scout had proved himself the better man.

Cole stood rigid, hardening himself, resolved not to interfere. Whatever the Shawnee had in store for Cairns, it was going to be a lot worse than hanging from an army rope.

He tramped back to where he found Lester. There were several Confederate corpses nearby, a testament to the fight the

Englishman had put up before he, too, was killed. Kneeling next to him, Cole found a paper balled up in the man's fist. Taking it and reading it, he discovered it to be the hasty outline of the plan Lester had unearthed back at the camp, detailing, albeit briefly, Jeb Stuart's strategy.

After resting and drinking from his canteen, Cole much later came upon the two young troopers who had obediently waited for his return. They were full of questions but, having taken one look at Cole's expression, they decided to remain silent.

And, it was in silence that they rode back to the Union camp where Cole went to Major Knowles and, without a word, placed Lester's plan on the officer's desk. And, it was in silence that Cole retired to the bunkhouse, stretched himself out and slept for the rest of that day and most of the following one.

He woke, refreshed, filled with a new determination. The horrors of the past months he would store away, not to forget, but rather, learn to live with. He put all his energies into his life as an army scout, steeling himself, focusing on his duties, becoming single-minded in his quest to be the most resourceful and successful tracker there was. The war would help him, mould him and allow him to develop every talent he might need, now and for the rest of his life.

CHAPTER TWENTY

Cole led a patrol out into the wilderness. News of raids on outlying farmsteads caused a good deal of concern. His quarry, however, proved elusive, and it was with great reluctance he made his way back to the fort. It was upon his return that he heard of Antietam and the terrible loss of life the battle caused. He spent several days kicking his heels as more and more reports trickled in. It seemed that all of his efforts to bring Cairns to justice and return Lester's plans had been for nothing. The Army of the Potomac licked its wounds, but overall victory was some way off.

Then, the morning came when all soldiers were assembled on the parade ground, battle standards unfurled, officers in full dress. Cole stood a little detached, the chill air biting deep through his clothes. Winter was making itself felt.

Major Knowles lifted his voice to read from the letter in his hands. Lincoln had done it, as many always believed he would. His Emancipation Proclamation struck a chord with all those who believed the war was fought for more than just the continuation of the Union – it was about common decency and the undoubted right of all human beings to be free.

Later, as they sat around drinking in the camp saloon, Cole was summoned to the Major's quarters.

"Cole," said Knowles, chomping on a cigar, his back to the scout as Cole waited ramrod still, "I'm sending you out again." He turned. His face was set, mouth a thin line. "Another family has been attacked. Parents and sons murdered, daughters carried off to God knows what fate. It seems they waited for your return before launching this assault."

"That means they were keeping us under observation, sir."

"Or, that someone had told them of your movements."

Blinking, Cole rocked back slightly on his heels. "An informer, sir? Here in the camp? I thought we'd got rid of them all. After Cairns—"

"Indeed. But, it would appear that we still have Reb infiltrators amongst us. They're feeding the enemy information, perhaps in the erroneous belief that the Confederacy can win this war."

"After the inconclusive outcome at Antietam, perhaps that belief has more followers than it had before."

Frowning, Knowles went to his desk. "Yesterday, a body was discovered. Murdered. The perpetrator had slit the man's throat and hidden the body under a mountain of straw in one of the hay barns."

It took a moment for these revelations to sink in, and Cole, struggling to make sense of them, shook his head, reached for a chair and sat down. Almost immediately, he realised he had done so without asking permission and went to stand, blurting, "Apologies, Major, I—"

"At ease, Cole," said Knowles as he lowered himself into the chair opposite the scout. "This has come as a shock to all of us."

"But, who was it, sir? A drunken dispute perhaps? Even so, it's rare for our boys to settle scores with the blade of a knife."

"No, it was some drunken brawl, Cole. It was Corporal Simmonds. You know him? He was a US Marshall back in the late fifties in one of those rough towns in Kansas. It was because of his qualifications that I chose him to investigate."

"Investigate? The identity of the spy, you mean?"

Knowles grunted and nodded. "Seems he was too good at his job. Whoever he'd unmasked silenced him for good."

"Then, I'll take it upon myself to uncover him. I'll ride out, investigate what happened in the latest homestead attack, then circle back to see if I can uncover whoever it is who's giving the raiders the information they need."

Without a word, Knowles swung around and opened the door to a large, glass-fronted cabinet. He selected a bottle and two glasses. "You drink, Cole?"

Readjusting himself in the chair, Cole cleared his throat a little self-consciously, "No, sir. I do not."

"Wise man," said Knowles, and poured himself a generous measure. "This is French cognac. The finest there is. I find it brings me a calmness of mind." He smiled, raised his glass, and then downed the contents in one. Eyes closed, luxuriating in the effects of the alcohol, he breathed, "Damn fine."

"I'll leave at once," said Cole, getting to his feet. He saluted, turned, and left. It was only when he was again outside that he stopped, drew in a huge breath, and released a long, shuddering sigh. He felt sure that the Major's drinking would be the death of him.

He was almost right.

CHAPTER TWENTY-ONE

It proved surprisingly easy to pick up the tracks. Perhaps too easy. The three chosen men in his squad chewed on grass, breathed hard, and waited with a distinct lack of patience as Cole, down on his knees, studied the ground.

"Cole, they is close," said one of the men, crossing his leg to rest behind the saddle pommel as he rolled himself a cigarette. "All we need do is swing wide and fast, come at them from the flank, and blow them the hell away."

"That's right, Cole," said another. "What in the hell are we waitin' for?"

"Christmas," said the third, and they all laughed.

Standing up, Cole fixed his gaze at the distant horizon. "Something's not right."

"Ah, damn it, Cole," said the one with the cigarette. He lit it, drew in a lungful of smoke, "it's as easy as easy is."

"That's just it, Todd," said Cole, crossing to his horse. He carefully pulled out the Luttich from the scabbard. "The tracks are too damned neat. Almost as if they've been deliberately set here to..."

"To what?" Todd chuckled to himself and released a long

stream of smoke. "You been out on your own for too long, Cole. You scared of your own damned shadow!"

Another chorus of laughter followed. Ignoring them, Cole pointed towards a line of trees. "We'll head over there, make camp, set up a defensive ring. Then, we keep watch until—"

"We have hours until sundown," said the second scout. "I reckon we should fan out in a line, look for signs and move real slow until we come upon them."

"Or, we simply veer off towards the homestead those bastards torched," interjected the third. "Either way, it beats holing up somewhere like a bunch of prairie dogs."

"He's right," said Todd. "Fights are only ever won if we take it to the enemy, Cole. You should know that."

"Even if we can't see our enemy?"

"Shoot, Cole," spat the third scout, "I volunteered to run down Reb scavengers, not sit on my fat and hairy ass waiting for 'em to come a-callin'!" He drew his pistol and checked the load. "Let's ride across to the homestead, pick up their trail, and beat them to hell and back!"

The others whooped and cheered, swinging their mounts to face the east. "You comin', Cole?"

"No, I ain't, Staines, and if you want my advice, you won't either." He kicked at the ground. "This is all too damned easy..."

"Come on," said Staines. "We'll see you on the way back."

"Never took you for yella, Cole."

Cole flashed the second scout a dangerous look. "Watch your mouth, Davies. You're riding into a whole mess of trouble. If you have any sense, you'll do as I say and not go running blind into what is clearly a trap."

Davies smirked, kicked his horse, and galloped off, Todd and Staines falling swiftly behind him. Cole stood and watched them until they were nothing but a smudge of dust in the distance. Then, blowing out his breath, he led his horse across to the trees and found himself a place to settle down and wait.

———

The effective range of the Luttich carbine, so he'd been reliably informed, was a good six hundred paces. Some reports, mentioned by British troops during the Crimean War, spoke of over a thousand. Cole couldn't trust this latter figure, so when the riders first appeared, he patiently waited, flicking up the rear sight, and calibrating it to five hundred. He needed to make every shot count.

There were five of them. It must have been as he suspected. The Rebs had waited at the homestead and ambushed Todd and the others using the false trail as a lure. Why hadn't the others accepted his words? Why had they argued so vehemently against such good sense? If they had been forced to do so, to obey orders, the outcome would have proved a lot better. But then, Cole could not order anyone. He did not have the authority, the rank. He was like them, a private. The lowest of the low. Something would have to change if he was to continue in this role.

He peered through the sight. The riders were still a little out of range. He turned and pulled out the German binoculars he so cherished. Adjusting the glasses, the riders sprung up in perfect focus.

He sucked in a breath, unable to believe what he saw.

"It can't be," he said to himself. Scrambling to his feet, he hastily gathered together his few belongings, mounted up and gingerly led his horse away from the prairie, threading a path through the trees. As soon as he was free of them, he kicked his horse into a gallop and raced back to the fort.

What he'd seen shocked him beyond imagination. But now, armed with this chilling knowledge, he needed to tell Knowles as quickly as possible. The infiltrator, the spy, the *traitor* now exposed could be brought to justice at last.

CHAPTER TWENTY-TWO

There was turmoil in the fort when Cole returned, men scurrying around like they were in a frantic search for something. Lots of shouting, barking sergeants issuing orders. Cole caught sight of a bedraggled orderly emerging from the telegraph office, clutching a sheet of paper, eyes glued to it as if nothing there made any sense. He came to an abrupt halt in front of Cole and spluttered, "Army's fallen back. McClellan is being replaced. Dear God Almighty, it's chaos. What is with the Major an' all? This is just a disaster..." He continued on his way, stomping up the stairs of the Major's quarters. Cole watched him and, more confused than ever, stood dazed and speechless on the parade ground.

"Cole?" came a voice, rough, deep, not to be ignored. "Cole, is that you?"

Turning, Cole was pleased to see the big, dependable form of Sergeant Burnside striding towards him.

"It's good to see you after so long," said the young scout.

"You found them, Cole? You found the raiders?"

"I did, indeed. And, a darn sight more besides. I have to report to Major Knowles and inform him of—"

"Something terrible has happened."

"Terrible?" Cole looked again towards the major's quarters, the men running in and out, the confused, agitated state of everyone around.

"Major Knowles was found dead this morning."

Reeling backwards, as if struck by a great weight slamming into his chest, Cole gagged, finding it hard to breathe. He spluttered, "I... I don't understand. Dead? Was it, was he... Damn it all... was it the drink that killed him?"

"The drink? What the hell! No! He was murdered, Cole. Somebody put a knife into his throat. Not just once, either. Maybe he was drunk when it happened 'cause there don't seem to be any signs of a struggle. Anyways, Lieutenant Pace is now the acting commander as no one, not even his wife, can find head-nor-tail of Captain Randall. He may have—"

"Sergeant," Cole shot out his hands and gripped Burnside by the lapels, "that's what I wanted to speak to the Major about. We were lured into a trap. The raiders, I reckon, ambushed and killed the rest of the group. They wouldn't listen to me and they rode off straight into it..."

"Cole," Burnside pointedly nodded to Cole's hands holding his jacket. Realising what he was doing, Cole gasped and dropped his hands, muttering his apologies. "Tell me again, son. The others of your squad. They're dead?"

"I'm guessing so. I didn't see any of it. They rode off after a trail we'd picked up. But, this is the truth of it, Sergeant. That trail, it was deliberately set to lure us into that ambush. I tried to tell 'em, tried to put some sense into their heads, but they wouldn't listen. They rode off and that was the last I saw of 'em."

"But, you can't be sure they're dead, Cole. How could you—?"

"I'm coming to it, Sarge. I remained behind because I knew... either ways, the next thing is, those raiders came charging down on me like a pack of wild hounds. I shot a couple of 'em with my Luttich, but I had to get out of there before I was overrun. I shook 'em off and made it back here." Cole's eyes grew moist and he couldn't stop himself from dragging the back of one hand across his face. "One of 'em, Sarge, the one in the lead... It was Captain Randall."

"*Randall?* Are you sure?"

"As sure as I'm standing here."

"But... but how can that be? I think we need to..." Burnside turned, lifted his voice and barked across to a group of soldiers lingering outside Major Knowles's quarters. "Private! Go and fetch Lieutenant Pace and tell him to—"

"He's inside, Sarge."

"Damn it all..." Burnside sucked in a huge breath. "We need to inform the Lieutenant. He'll want to hear what you have to say."

Less than a quarter of an hour later, Lieutenant Pace, having steered Cole and Burnside away from the clamour surrounding the Major's quarters, listened intently to the recounting of what happened with Cole and his pursuit by Randall and the raiders. He stood in silence, hands on hips, chewing on a plug of tobacco, staring at the ground. As soon as Cole finished his story, Pace spat out a long line of brown juice, readjusted his trousers, and gave the young scout a lingering look.

"That's all very interesting... Cole, is it?"

The scout nodded, the first unsettling tingling developing around the nape of his neck.

"So, where are they?"

Cole frowned, wrong-footed by this question. "Where are who, sir?"

"The raiders you say charged after you? What happened to them?"

Cole shot a quick puzzled glance towards Burnside before he returned to the Lieutenant's penetrating glare. "Like I told you, sir, I lost 'em in the woods before I—"

"Yes, before you returned here to inform us of this curious turn of events."

"Curious? Sir, Captain Randall was in cahoots with the raiders! That's how they knew which farms to attack, which ones weren't defended or visited by our men."

"And, the Major?"

"Sir? I don't quite understand..."

"He was murdered, Cole. How do you explain that? If the Captain was part of this raiding group, then who killed Major Knowles? Another infiltrator? Or, *Mrs* Randall, perhaps?"

"Sir, I never would believe that Mrs Ra—"

"No, of course not. The Major's murder was brutal and violent. No woman, certainly not one of Mrs Randall's good standing, could have wielded a knife with such uncontained ferocity." Pace shook his head. "We only have your word for what you've told us, Cole. Fortunately, for you, all the others are missing and presumed dead."

Cole's mouth fell open. "Sir, you can't be accusing me of—"

"I'm not accusing you of anything, Cole. Not yet. Sergeant, order some men to escort Cole to the fort jail where he will wait until my investigations are complete."

Cole stammered, "But, sir, what I've told you is the truth, and if there is another infiltrator in the camp, then we need to find him."

"Indeed, we do, Cole. Sergeant, conduct this scout to the jail."

CHAPTER TWENTY-THREE

They stripped Cole of his guns, knife, and belt before leading him unceremoniously to the jail. More than a hundred accusing faces turned to him and watched as he, together with his escort, crossed the parade ground. Cole dare not meet any of the stares. Each was so full of suspicion, even hatred. His heart sank, and a dreadful, dark cloud settled over him. Even when the solid clang of the jail door closing behind him caused him to jump, he could not summon up the strength to speak out. Everything was out of control, a mad kaleidoscope of mixed emotion, bewilderment and half, ill-thought-out questions whirling around in his brain. He could make no sense of what was happening, or why. Nobody believed him, not even Burnside. In despair, he fell onto his bunk and, face in hands, fought to calm his jangled nerves.

Dog tired, he slept. But, no sooner had his eyes closed than the front door of the jailhouse crashed open and he sat up, heart pounding, alive with fear.

Burnside, so big he seemed to fill the room, gestured for the guard to open the cell.

"It's your lucky day, Cole," snapped the sergeant as the iron door swung open. Cole stood there, confused and worried, writing his hands, not sure if he should step forward or not.

"I don't understand."

"You'll see. Come with me."

It didn't take long for Cole to find himself standing in one of the bunkhouses, peering down at a bedraggled, sweat and blood-covered individual whose hands shook uncontrollably. He looked up and gasped when he recognised the young scout. "Oh my good God Almighty," he said, his voice breaking with emotion. He struggled to get to his feet.

"Staines?" Cole could hardly believe it. Without thinking, he took this shattered, former companion in his arms and held him as the man broke down and wept.

"He came in this morning on the back of a broken down old mule," explained Burnside. "No one recognised him at first, but hell, here he is... Private Joshua Staines, and he looks as if he has been to hell and back. He has certainly got a fever."

Nodding, Cole helped lower the man down onto the bunk bed once more. He got down on his knees and waited for Staines to recover.

"He has been mumbling about being ambushed, the others dying, how he played dead before finding that old mule and making it back here. What he says, it backs up your story, Cole."

"Have you told Lieutenant Pace?"

A dark look came over the big sergeant. "The Lieutenant has left the fort, Cole. I went across to inform him of Staines' arrival and found his quarters empty. I spoke with the sentries and they told me the lieutenant rode out early, maybe an hour after Staines turned up."

Shaking his head, Cole turned again to Staines. "Josh, can you tell me what happened?"

"We... Cole, we should've listened to you. What you said about them signs, you spoke such good sense. If Davies had..." He dragged in a shuddering breath.

"Don't fret none about what should and shouldn't have happened. What's done is done, Josh. Just tell it."

"We rode in, thinking to catch 'em unawares, but it was them that did so to us! We found the cabin, the little farmhouse, empty. No one about. And, as we searched, they came upon us like ghosts... I tell you, we never even heard 'em until Todd took the first shot in his head. We tried, we did what we could, emptied our pistols into 'em, but they just kept coming... and Cole, one of 'em was the Captain." He looked up to Burnside. "Captain Randall. He seemed to be the one in charge. He was the one who shot Davies. Then, I got this one in my arm," he turned his right arm over to show how the blood had soaked through his sleeve. "It won't stop bleeding. I tried to bandage it up, but I don't think I've done it right."

"We'll get it looked at," said Cole, squeezing Staines' good hand. "You did well, Josh. You've got me out of a fix."

"I'm glad of that, Cole. We should have followed what you said, but we didn't, and now we're all dead."

"Not you, Josh. We'll get you fixed up, so don't you worry none."

"I played dead, Cole. It was the only thing I could do. I got this bullet in my arm. The force of it threw me to the ground, and I thought why not just lay here and wait it all out. So, I did, and when they left, I made my way here. I know it was cowardly of me, but I'd seen the others die and I didn't want no part of that, Cole. No part at all."

Staines broke down again, this time, the sobbing so total nothing that Cole did caused it to subside. After several moments, reluctantly, Cole stood and nodded across to Burnside. "I'll go after Pace. Bring him back. He must face justice."

"You think he's the infiltrator?"

"He has to be. I also think he was the one who murdered the Major. In the confusion, him taking over command, we can only guess at what his next move might have been."

"You can't go out there on your own, Cole. It's suicide."

"Sarge, I've already been responsible for the deaths of too many good men. This time, it's down to me."

"I can't let you do that, son. Take Arnoldson. He's true and dependable and one helluva soldier. I'll order him to the livery where you can find two fresh horses."

"All right, but make him move quick – I'll be leavin' within the half-hour."

Something was not right.

Standing outside the front door to Mrs Randall's residence, waiting for her to respond to his knocking, Cole, having pressed his ear close to the woodwork to listen, stepped back and drew his gun. Had she, in fact, fled along with Pace, to join her husband? Was she part of the network of enemy spies who were doing their utmost to undermine and weaken the fort's garrison and leave it open to attack? He recalled her reaction to the death of Penny and her family. Surely, Mrs Randall could not have faked such an outpouring of grief?

Recalling Penny stopped him for a moment. Her lovely face loomed up from the corners of his memory. Murdered. How many deaths was he responsible for? How many more before the tally grew so large that he would turn his back on this ghastly business, return to his father's ranch, become a cowboy and live a life without killing?

Steadying himself, he pushed such thoughts away, took a breath and kicked through the door, splintering the hinges from the doorframe with little trouble. The sound echoed loudly through the little house, but no response came from within. Cole stepped inside.

He waited, holding his breath, straining to listen. He noticed how cold the hallway was, how dark. The silence was tangible. As slowly as he could, he inched forward.

The little parlour where Mrs Randall had welcomed him in what seemed to Cole as a lifetime ago, seemed ordered, with little sign that anything had happened. He moved on, stopped outside the bedroom and gave a tentative knock.

He eased open the door and stood in the doorway, engaging the hammer on his gun. A trickle of sweat dripped down from his brow.

He looked inside and could not prevent himself from crying out.

Burnside came down the step and sat down next to Cole. "This is worse than I could have imagined."

"These people, the ones who did this," Cole jerked his head towards the open entrance's direction, "they are monsters, Sergeant. Why would they kill her like that?"

"Maybe because she was about to tell us their plans? Who knows? She struck me as a good and honest woman. But then," he traced a ragged line through the dirt with the point of his boot, "so did her husband. These Rebs are audacious, calculating and—"

"Ruthless."

"Aye, that, too."

"It's my fault. If I hadn't come calling, hadn't asked her about Penny, then none of this—"

"None of this is your fault, son," said Burnside, placing his hand on the young scout's shoulder.

"Whose fault is it, then? Are you going to tell me it's what happens during war, that innocents die, that humanity and common decency are forgotten? Is that it?"

"Just about."

"I don't buy that. Every person has choices. That doesn't just disappear, locked away inside a box and the key thrown away. We all know what's right and what's wrong. What has happened here is wrong, war or no war. Mrs Randall, Penny, her family, all those farmsteaders, there was no reason for them to die."

Pressing a finger and thumb into his eyes, he waited for his anger to subside.

A shadow fell over him and a pair of dust-encrusted boots came into his line of sight. He looked up. A grim-faced private stood there, eyes flickering from Cole to Burnside. He stiffened and saluted, "Begging your pardon, Sergeant..."

"What is it, son?"

The private pulled a face. "I'm sorry to report Mr Burnside, sir, but—"

"You still call me Sergeant, son. I know I'm the most senior rank left in this place, but even so ..."

"Yes, sir – I mean *Sergeant*. It's Mr Staines, sir."

Cole snapped his head up. "Staines? What about him?"

"It's, er, his arm, you see. Mr Shipman, the medical orderly, he did his best, but it seems..." He swallowed hard.

"Get it out, son," said Burnside, his voice cold.

"His wound had gone gangrenous, Mr Shipman said, and there was nothing he could do but cut it off."

"Dear God," muttered Cole, and let his face fall once again.

Burnside sucked in a breath, "This never ends. How is he, son?"

"Well, that's just it, Mr Burnside. He's not."

"Not? Not what?"

"Not anything, Sergeant. Mr Shipman did his best, but the poor man, he just couldn't take it. He died, Sergeant, right there on the operating table. His heart I guess. It gave out."

Without a word, Cole stood up. He nodded to the private before turning his gaze to the open gates of the fort. Next to them, he could just make out the towering frame of Arnoldson standing there with two horses.

"I'll get going, Sarge. I don't want to tarry here any longer."

"Cole, bring him back alive." He squeezed his lips together, "If you can."

"Yeah. If I can."

CHAPTER TWENTY-FOUR

Cole lay prone, Arnoldson close by, the horses some way off, munching at tufts of prairie grass. They were blown, the relentless urging of Cole bringing them close to the point of collapse. But now, all was calm. The trail proved easy to pick out. Pace, anxious to put as much distance as he could between himself and the fort, had thoughtlessly ridden his horse across the rolling plains, trampling down a path through the grass, an unmistakeable directional sign that anyone could follow.

"You won't hit him from here," grunted Arnoldson. He was peering through Cole's field glasses.

"This has a range of a thousand," said Cole, adjusting the Luttich's calibrated sight. "Let's see."

He held his breath. Aimed.

The single shot rang out across the prairie, shattering the stillness, causing the horses to scream and kick with fright.

Arnoldson let out a long sigh, lowered the glasses and said, "What now?"

Cole sat up. "I'd say we track Randall. Pace must have been heading his way, probably at some appointed rendezvous."

"They'll be waiting."

"At the same farmhouse where they killed Todd and Davies, I shouldn't wonder."

"So, you know the way?"

Cole nodded. "We'll ease our way there, and if they are there, we'll come upon them at night."

"And, Pace? What do we do with him?"

Cole did not look at the huge Sergeant, the man who had taught him so much. "Coyotes, buzzards? They all need a good breakfast, wouldn't you say?"

"I never thought you'd become so cold. You've changed a lot since you dumped me in the dirt."

"I guess so." He took to methodically reloading the carbine. "His horse, we'll pick it up, take it with us."

"You do it. I'll make my way towards the farm. I'll be walking so you won't have no trouble following."

They camped without making a fire. In the slight dip, the farmhouse stood. At any other time, the sight would have been a welcoming one, the smoke gently trailing from the chimney top, a cosy orange glow filtering out from the windows. Cole, however, knew the truth of what waited inside.

"We go in hard," said Cole. "You stand at the rear, shoot anyone who manages to come out. If you see Randall, you wing him. He's mine."

"Cole, this isn't what Burnside wanted. Bring 'em in alive is what he said."

"If you don't like this, Arnoldson, wait here. You said earlier I've changed. Well, damned right I have. Those people inside? They murdered Penny. And Randall, he killed his own wife. I ain't gonna forgive any of that, you hear me? I'm putting them in the ground and that is that."

Arnoldson did not offer a reply. Instead, he brought out his gun and, together with Cole, moved across the open space. Guided by the burning light of the farmhouse, their approach was simple enough and, as Arnoldson slipped to the rear of the building, Cole positioned himself two dozen paces or so from the main door. He waited, brought the Luttich up to his shoulder, and squeezed off a round through the open window. He then placed the carbine aside.

All hell broke loose from that point, several terrified voices shouting from inside. Two men burst through the door, dressed in grubby underwear, guns drawn.

Cole, too, had both of his guns ready.

He shot down those two men, blasting one of them back inside.

Sprinting forward, Cole went through the door in a roll. He took in the confusion around him. There were three of them in various stages of undress, struggling to find firearms. Another tore open the rear door and ran outside. Cole heard the satisfying roar of Arnoldson's big Colt Walker blowing the raider apart.

Cole shot two of the others from where he knelt, then paused as his eyes fell upon Randall.

Up until that point, Cole had only seen Randall from a distance, and had never spoken to him. But now, here he was, a short man, deeply etched face, large, handlebar moustache and greased back hair worn long.

"You..." muttered Randall.

"You killed your own wife," said Cole through gritted teeth.

"She was no wife to me," the former captain said and went for his gun.

Cole continued to fire until the hammers fell on empty cylinders and Randall lay still, his chest perforated with gunshot holes, the blood seeping out across the wooden floor.

Coming through the backdoor at a rush, Arnoldson blew out a loud breath. "Dear God..."

"We'll torch the place," said Cole, holstering his guns. "We don't want this unhappy place to remain a centre for Reb activity."

Grunting, Arnoldson acquiesced and took to preparing the various sticks of furniture in jumbled piles. He took the lamp oil and placed drenched pieces of cloth strategically here and there.

"The bodies?"

Cole shook his head and turned away. "Just burn the whole stinking lot."

Burnside found Cole standing, head bowed, in front of Penny's grave. The sun had come out, chasing away the chill of the morning. Cole acknowledged him, and together, they strolled away from the small cemetery towards the fort.

"Army is repositioning," said Burnside. "My namesake has replaced McClellan. Major-General Burnside." He chuckled, "No relation, I'm sorry to add."

At the fort, Burnside stopped. "I, myself, am being promoted. Second-Lieutenant. It's quite an honour. My good wife is as happy as punch and is already deciding on a new dinner service to buy so we can entertain."

"Congratulations."

He reached inside his jacket and produced an envelope. "Hope you can sew, Cole."

"Sew? What do you mean?"

Burnside handed over the envelope. Cole tore it open and sighed. "I don't want this."

"It's not just as a recognition of your bravery, Cole, it's more of a surety against any future questioning of your decisions. Like you've always said, if those men had obeyed your orders, they might well be alive."

"But, we might not have uncovered just who was plotting against us."

"Regardless, Cole, you're a corporal now. So, get those stripes sewn on and report to me as soon as you're done. You have work to do."

Burnside saluted and Cole returned it, although he did not

raise his head. As the newly promoted Lieutenant marched off, Cole fingered the corporal stripes and wondered what his mother would think. She'd be proud, he knew that. For himself, however, the thought filled him with dread.

THE END OF PART TWO

Dear reader,

We hope you enjoyed reading *Army Days*. Please take a moment to leave a review, even if it's a short one. Your opinion is important to us.

Discover more books by Stuart G. Yates at
https://www.nextchapter.pub/authors/stuart-g-yates

Want to know when one of our books is free or discounted? Join the newsletter at
http://eepurl.com/bqqB3H

Best regards,

Stuart G. Yates and the Next Chapter Team

ABOUT THE AUTHOR

The Luttich carbine was a Russian percussion rifle, copied in 1843 from the British Brunswick rifle. Used extensively in the Crimean War, it became the bane of British troops due to its long range. Its rear sight is graduated to 1200 paces, a remarkable distance for a weapon of this time. It is, therefore, not inconceivable that in the hands of a trained sharpshooter, it could hit a target at one thousand paces, which is exactly what Cole did when he blew Pace out of his addle in this story!

Army Days
ISBN: 978-4-86751-646-1

Published by
Next Chapter
1-60-20 Minami-Otsuka
170-0005 Toshima-Ku, Tokyo
+818035793528

17th October 2021